GRITS & GRIEVANCES

The Jubilee Series, Book 5

CHAPTER 1

W alter Cooper pulled his old pickup truck up to the usual parking spot in front of his longtime restaurant, Coop's Home Cookin'. His back was still aching from picking up big bags of flour the day before. As he got out of the driver's seat, he took a deep breath of the cool mountain air, hoping it would clear his mind and somehow heal his rapidly aging body. Coop's Home Cookin' was more than just a local diner. It was the heartbeat of Jubilee, as far as he was concerned. For over forty years, he had been its owner and keeper, watching his neighbors come and go and their families grow up. Little kids that had sat in high chairs at one point were now having kids of their own. Locals gathered there for their morning cups of coffee and eggs just the way they liked them.

He removed his baseball cap and wiped the sweat off his head. He used to have so much more hair up there, but time had stolen it away. He put his hat back on and looked at the storefront across the street. It had been empty for over a year, a sad reminder that sometimes small towns struggled to keep businesses afloat. Previously, it was a gift shop, but today, something looked different. Construction workers were bustling around, hammering and sawing, setting up what looked like a new awning. He squinted to get a better look, but his eyes weren't what they used to be. A banner flapped in the wind, and he could finally make out the words: *Coming Soon: Jubilee Vegan Café.* It was scrawled in neat, modern lettering.

"Jubilee Vegan Café," he muttered under his breath, his brows pulling together as he tried to make sense of it. A vegan café? This wasn't some big city, and Jubilee didn't need some newfangled café that served overpriced, dainty, tasteless salads and special tea. He shook his head, feeling irritation flare up in his chest. *Jubilee Vegan Café* sounded suspiciously like one of those modern joints where people ate tofu and avocado toast instead of a proper breakfast of bacon and eggs.

As he crossed the street, he could see more details: clean, minimalist décor inside, sleek light fixtures, and a new glossy white counter being installed. Everything about this place rubbed him the wrong way, with its polished modern edges clashing against the cozy charm of Jubilee.

Just then, some construction workers noticed he was standing there staring. They exchanged looks with each other as if they knew exactly who he was, the man who kept Jubilee's diner running since before they could even remember. Coop could feel them looking at him, but he didn't bother to look away. This was *his* town, after all.

The bell above the door jingled as he walked inside the diner. As usual, the smell of coffee and fresh biscuits greeted him, soothing him slightly. At least Coop's Home Cookin' was exactly as it had always been. No fuss, no frills. There was no need to fix what wasn't broken.

"Morning, Coop," a regular named Jimmy called from his usual spot at the counter. He was drinking his cup of coffee, probably his third or fourth by now, his trucker cap tilted back as he watched the news on a small old TV in the corner.

"Morning, Jimmy," Coop said with a nod. He made his way to the back but couldn't shake the thought of that place across the street.

By the time he reached the kitchen, his mind was racing. What in the world did Jubilee need with a vegan restaurant? He could picture it now—a bunch of city folks coming up there, ordering their almond milk lattes and kale salads, sticking their noses up at his hearty breakfasts that he'd been serving for decades. He prided himself on knowing every face that came through his doors, knowing all of their stories, and the thought of losing even a single customer to some hip new café made his stomach churn.

He grabbed a dish towel and wiped his hands more aggressively than necessary, and then Wanda, one of his longtime waitresses, walked in with her black and silver hair pulled back into a bun and her apron dotted with flour from making biscuits. Her deep, smooth complexion hid the fact that she was only about ten years younger than Coop. Of course, Wanda rarely ate their food, choosing to bring her own from home. She said her health was more important than fried eggs and cheesy grits.

"Coop, what's got you lookin' like a storm cloud this early?" she asked, looking at him over her thick glasses.

He pointed toward the window. "Have you seen what they're putting up across the street?"

She peered out and shrugged. "The new café? I did. It's like a vegan place or something."

He grunted. "Yeah, Jubilee Vegan Café," he

replied, his words dripping with sarcasm. "Can you believe that nonsense? What's wrong with good down-home cooking?"

Wanda chuckled. "Maybe it'll bring some new faces to town, Coop. That could be good for business."

He shook his head. "Good for *their* business, maybe, but folks who come to a place like this, well, they're not looking for biscuits and gravy or country ham. They'll want salads with that quinoa stuff or whatever's trendy this week. They're trying to be hip and cool, and they won't ever come to visit a diner like this."

She rolled her eyes, nudging him with her elbow. "Oh, hush. People around here have been eating at Coop's for years, and they're going to keep coming. You might even get curious people wanting to come over here and see what this place is all about."

He knew she was probably right, but he couldn't shake the frustration. The diner was who he was. It was his identity, and the thought of some flashy café taking business from him with their fancy menus and modern décor just didn't sit right.

Wanda must have seen his jaw tighten because she added, "Why don't you go on over there and introduce yourself? Show them who runs things around here."

He snorted. "Not likely. If they don't know already, they'll find out soon enough." He tossed the dish towel onto the counter and walked up front to greet each of his customers by name.

As he filled their coffee cups and took orders, he couldn't help but look across that street as more construction workers brought in sleek booths and glossy fixtures. He'd spent his lifetime building this diner from the ground up, and the thought of anyone taking business away made his grip on the coffee pot tighten.

Jimmy finished his coffee and waved him over. "So, Coop, you think that café is going to steal your thunder?" he teased.

Coop grunted, pouring him another refill. "Steal my thunder? I don't think so. Very unlikely. But I'll tell you one thing: ain't nobody coming to Jubilee to eat food they can't even pronounce."

Jimmy chuckled, taking a sip. "I don't know, Coop. I heard the guy who owns it is some chef from the city. Might be big competition."

Coop's eyes narrowed. "Competition? We'll see about that."

The day wore on, and as the lunch crowd filled the booths, Coop could feel his irritation bubbling under the surface. Jubilee Vegan Café. If they wanted to bring a fight to his doorstep, he'd lace up his boxing gloves and be ready.

T he lunch crowd at Coop's Home Cookin' had settled, leaving a few stragglers drinking their sweet teas and lemonade, swapping stories at the counter. Coop leaned back against the counter, a towel over his shoulder, lost in thought. He couldn't stop staring out the window at the sign across the street: *Jubilee Vegan Café.* Just seeing it there felt like a challenge.

As he was gathering coffee cups, he saw his daughter Whitney slip into the diner, looking, as always, fresh-faced and bright in her work scrubs. She was a nurse at the local clinic, a job that kept her very busy but brought her into Coop's every after-noon like clockwork. She walked over, and he gave her a quick smile as she slid onto one of the stools at the counter.

"Hey, Daddy," she greeted. "You look like you've seen a ghost. What's going on?"

"Worse than seeing a ghost," he muttered, pouring her a glass of sweet tea and putting it in front of her. "I've seen a vegan café."

She laughed, taking a sip of her tea. "Oh, you mean the new place across the street?"

He grunted, crossing his arms. "Yeah, *Jubilee Vegan Café*, or whatever they're calling it. What in the world does this town need with a vegan café?"

She gave him an amused look, putting a loose strand of hair behind her ear. "Maybe it's not such a bad thing, Daddy. People might actually like it. We could do with some more healthy foods around here. It could bring in a different crowd, though. Maybe even get more folks into Jubilee."

He raised an eyebrow, unimpressed with her optimism. "More folks? And what exactly do you think these new folks are gonna be looking for? Kale smoothies? Tofu?" He shook his head. "This is Jubilee, not Atlanta."

She rolled her eyes. "I'm just saying it might bring some life into town, and who knows, people might try it out and then wander over here when they want to eat a hearty meal."

He gave her a skeptical look. "Oh, right. They're gonna come in here after paying a fortune for some lettuce leaves. This town's done just fine without some highfalutin café, Whitney. Folks here know what they like, and that's real food."

Whitney leaned her elbows on the counter. "Maybe some of us wouldn't mind trying something new every now and then. Not everybody wants biscuits and gravy every day, Daddy."

He scoffed, folding his arms tighter across his chest. "Oh, really? Well, they've done everybody well for many years now. If you want some tiny portions of who-knows-what for lunch, you're welcome to go on over there and see how it suits you."

She shook her head, hiding a smile. "I swear, Daddy, you're as stubborn as a mule. Times change. Sometimes that means new things come along, and you don't have to like it, but maybe just give it a chance."

He leaned forward. "Let me tell you something, Whit. I've been keeping this place going for over forty years. My customers are like family to me. I know what they like, and I sure as heck know it's not tofu. I'm not about to let that fancy café come waltzing in here like it owns the place."

"You sure are obsessed with tofu," Whitney said, laughing as she took another sip of her tea. "That café isn't gonna take over the town. Who knows? Maybe it'll even help your business. You could get new folks in here. People who might not have even come up to Jubilee otherwise."

He made a dismissive sound, shaking his head. "You sound like Wanda. Well, I'll believe it when I see it."

She reached across the counter, putting a gentle hand on his arm. "Look, I know how much Coop's Home Cookin' means to you, but maybe it's okay that Jubilee progresses a little. I mean, wouldn't it be nice to see some new faces up here?"

He looked at her, his jaw clenched. "I don't like it, Whit. Feels like Jubilee's changing right under my nose."

She squeezed his arm gently. "Change isn't always bad, Daddy. And besides, no café is gonna take away your customers. Coop's is one-of-a-kind, and everybody knows it."

"Yeah, well, we'll see, but I'm telling you, I don't have a good feeling about that place. You mark my words."

Whitney laughed, sliding off the stool. "I'll mark 'em, and I'll be back here to remind you the first time one of your customers wanders over there for a healthy meal." She leaned over the counter and gave him a quick peck on the cheek. "Now stop worrying and get back to what you're good at—feeding people."

He let out a reluctant laugh as he watched her leave. She paused in the doorway, giving him a small, knowing smile before stepping back onto the sidewalk. He watched her cross the street and noticed that she glanced at the new café on her way back to the clinic.

Coop sighed, feeling the weight of her words lingering. He couldn't shake the nagging thought that maybe she was right. Maybe he was too set in his ways, but he would never admit it out loud.

The door swung closed, and he glanced back out the window, frowning at seeing more construction trucks unloading equipment across the street. His grip tightened on the dish towel in his hand. Whatever it took, he was determined to keep Coop's Home Cookin' at the heart of Jubilee, even if it meant going up against some hotshot café.

Late afternoon had rolled around, and Coop was still grumbling to himself about the new vegan café when he suddenly heard a knock on the diner's door. He looked up from his spot behind the counter and saw a tall man, maybe in his early thirties, dressed in jeans and a button-down shirt that looked a little too crisp for Jubilee. The man pushed the door open, a friendly smile on his face, as he stepped inside.

Coop knew right away who this must be. He didn't even need an introduction.

The man held out his hand, his smile bright. "Hey there, you must be Coop. I'm Tate Morgan. I'm the one opening the café across the street."

Coop stared at him and his hand hanging in midair, but made no move to shake it. Instead, he crossed his arms over his broad chest, his expression tight.

"Yeah, I figured you were the one," he said, looking him up and down.

Tate's hand hung in the air for a second longer before he dropped it, his smile faltering a bit. He looked around the diner, taking in the worn leather booths, the vintage memorabilia hanging all over the walls, and the warm smell of coffee that lingered in the air.

"Nice place you've got here," he said. "Jubilee's lucky to have a spot like this. It's got some real character."

Coop grunted. "Been around a long time."

Tate shifted, rubbing the back of his neck, clearly sensing Coop's discomfort. "I just wanted to come by and introduce myself. Listen, I'm not looking to step on anyone's toes. I know this town's got its own traditions and way of life."

Coop's eyes narrowed. "Oh, is that right? Because from where I'm standing, it sure seems like you're stepping on a few toes, mainly mine."

Tate's brow creased. "Look, I get it. A vegan café may not be the typical thing you'd expect for a town like Jubilee, but I'm hoping that I can add to what you've got here. Bring in new people. Give the locals something different."

"Different, huh?" Coop said, laced with sarcasm. "I don't think Jubilee needs different. Folks around here like what they like."

Tate held Coop's gaze. "Well, sometimes I think it's nice to shake things up a little. Give people some options, you know?"

"Options," Coop repeated. "People around here don't need options. They've got everything they need right here."

Tate nodded, taking a step back. He wasn't giving up his friendly demeanor. "I get it, Coop. I really do. I respect what you've built here as a fellow business-man. I just want the chance to build something, too. Something I think the people here might appreciate."

Coop's eyes narrowed. "Appreciate? I've been running this diner for over four decades, and I don't need some newcomer coming in here telling me what my folks would appreciate."

Tate's jaw finally tightened. He took a deep breath, still keeping his tone polite. "Look, I don't mean any disrespect. I just thought maybe we could work together since we're right across the street from each other. My place isn't coming to replace yours. It's just an option for people who might want it. I did a lot of research here, and one thing that was missing in this small mountain town was healthy options."

Coop snorted. "Well, we'll see about that. My people around here are loyal. Don't think they'll be running over there to eat your fancy lettuce and fake meat tacos."

Tate smiled. "Well, I guess time will tell."

They stood in silence for a moment, like they were sizing each other up. Coop's expression didn't change, his stare unflinching. Tate shifted a bit, glancing around the diner one more time.

"I guess I should probably get back over to the café," Tate said. "Still a lot of work to do before we open."

"Yeah," Coop said flatly. "I'm sure you've got lots of work to do."

Tate paused, like he was searching for something else to say. Nothing came to him, so he started toward the door. "Take care, Coop," he said before giving one final nod and stepping outside.

As soon as Tate was out of the restaurant, Coop let out a breath. He watched through the window as Tate crossed the street with his tall, thin body—probably from eating all that vegan food—returning to the café with a spring in his step. Coop found that to be a little too smug for his liking. He shook his head, picked up his dish towel again, and wiped down the counter with a little more force than necessary.

So that was the guy who thought he could just waltz into Jubilee and set up shop like he owned the place. Coop had been here before Tate Morgan was probably even born, and he wasn't going to let some city slicker change things just because he thought the town needed, quote, "options."

He looked around his diner, his eyes falling on the faded photos on the wall and the creased menus that had hardly changed in decades, and he thought about the loyal customers who filled his booths every day. This place was his life's work and his legacy, and he wasn't going to let anybody, especially some fancy café owner, take that away.

He didn't believe that Tate was here for honorable reasons. He was here to make as much money as possible, just like every other big city business person. He set his jaw with a newfound resolve. Jubilee might have room for a lot of things, but it didn't have room for some café that was trying to rewrite the town's story—not as long as Coop was around.

CHAPTER 2

M adeline and Brady strolled side by side into Coop's Home Cookin' as they did almost every morning. They moved as if they belonged together, with his arm resting around her shoulders. They had a comfortable closeness that came from just being deeply in sync with one another.

"Morning, lovebirds," Wanda said, smiling as she reached for the coffee pot. "Y'all want the usual?"

Madeline nodded and smiled, sliding into the booth with Brady beside her. "You know us too well, Wanda."

Wanda poured two steaming mugs and set them on the table with a wink. "I love having regulars who don't need a menu. It sure makes my job easier."

Brady laughed as he wrapped his hands around his mug and then looked at Wanda. "So, what's the word around town this week? You always know the best gossip."

Wanda raised an eyebrow with a mischievous grin, pulling at her lips. "Well, if you ask Coop, it's that Jubilee Vegan Café is going to be the end of this town. I swear he's going on and on about it to anybody who'll listen. People are trying to get away from him."

"A café?" Madeline said. "I hadn't noticed what was going in over there."

Wanda nodded, lowering her voice so that Coop couldn't hear her. "Yeah, and it's not just any café, a vegan one. I swear Coop's been calling it everything from a big-city invasion to a tragedy in Jubilee. You'd think they were setting up shop just to drive him out of business."

Brady chuckled. "Let me guess, he's convinced they're going to run him out of town with salads and smoothies?"

Wanda nodded, shaking her head. "You know him too well. He thinks the town has gone soft and says the next thing you know, we're going to be replacing fried chicken with tofu."

Madeline exchanged an amused look with Brady. "Well, I guess that's one idea," she said. "What do you think, Brady? Should we go see what all the fuss is about?"

He raised an eyebrow, entertained by the idea. "You think we should sneak over to the competition, Madeline?"

"Oh, not to eat there. They're not even open yet. I just want to see what's got Coop so riled up. It's hard to believe that little café could be such a threat."

Brady laughed, lifting her hand up to his lips for a quick kiss. "I suppose a little peek couldn't hurt. We better be careful, because if Coop catches us, we'll never hear the end of it. He's liable to poison our coffee next time."

Wanda topped off their mugs. "Now don't y'all go startin' trouble," she teased, "but if you ask me, Jubilee could use a little something new every now and then. It doesn't mean folks won't keep coming here, but nobody's convincing Coop of that."

"Sounds like you're the voice of reason around here, Wanda," Brady said.

She rolled her eyes, setting the coffee pot down. "Try telling that to Coop."

As she walked away, Madeline and Brady smiled at each other, their hands still linked together.

"Well, I guess Coop thinks he's got himself a real rival," Brady said, laughing.

"It seems silly to be so worked up, but I get it. He's been here forever. Sometimes people are just afraid of change."

"That's probably what it is," Brady agreed, looking around the diner. "But some things never change, and that's the part of Jubilee I love. This place hasn't changed a bit since I was in high school."

Brady changed the subject, talking about the latest things going on at the farm and how Gilbert wouldn't stop gnawing on the corner of the fence, and he would have to replace it pretty soon. She talked about the progress she was making with her newest book, and every now and then, his gaze would settle on her, and she'd see that quiet warmth in his eyes that made her feel like the only woman in the room.

They lingered over breakfast a bit, trying to have an easy start to the day. Wanda passed by again, giving them a knowing smile. "You two look too cozy in here. I might start charging y'all rent."

Madeline laughed. "What can I say? Every place in Jubilee feels like home."

Brady took her hand again, his thumb brushing over her knuckles. "And that's because it is, Madeline. As long as you're here, every place is home to me."

B rady and Madeline were finishing up their breakfast as they lingered over the last bits of biscuits and coffee. When Coop walked out of the kitchen, his face set in a deep scowl, he saw them in the booth by the window. Without missing a beat, he marched over and pulled up a chair, planting himself at their table.

"Well, look who's enjoying themselves this morning," he said. His gaze turned slightly to the window, where workers were painting a sign that said *Jubilee Vegan Café*. He was obviously distracted by it.

Madeline looked at Brady and then turned back to Coop with a smile. "Morning, Coop. Everything okay?"

"Okay? Hardly." Coop folded his arms across his chest, his frown deepening. He always wore one of those old-time white short-sleeved t-shirts that were so thin you could practically see his skin underneath it. "That pretentious restaurant over there has this whole town stirred up. Vegan this and vegan that. Who needs that kind of stuff?"

Brady bit back a grin. "Come on, Coop. Maybe it's not such a bad thing. It might bring some new people to Jubilee, and that's always a good thing."

"New people? Why does everybody keep saying that like it's a good thing? We don't need any more new people here," he muttered, rolling his eyes. "A bunch of city folks looking for fake burgers and green smoothies." He said the last part like it left a terrible taste in his mouth.

Madeline tried to remain neutral, stifling a smile as she took her final sip of coffee. "I think that café is just a little different, Coop. That's all. Maybe it's not your thing, but who knows? People might enjoy having a few options around here."

"Options. I've heard that before." Coop let out a heavy sigh and shook his head. "Well, if you ask me, folks around here don't need any options. They need the real food that God intended. Biscuits and gravy, bacon, eggs—food that sticks to your ribs." He patted his stomach, which was nowhere near his ribs. Coop hadn't seen his ribs in many years.

Brady leaned back. "Well, maybe you should just give it a try when it opens. Expand your palate a bit. You know, get out of your comfort zone."

Coop scoffed. "Expand my palate? No, thank you. I'll stick to the real food, Brady. I'm not about to swap my steak out for some fake beef nonsense."

"Come on, Coop," Madeline said. "Maybe you'll surprise yourself. Who knows? You could end up being a fan of quinoa."

"Quinoa," he repeated. "I wouldn't touch that stuff if you paid me. I don't know how you young folks eat it." He looked over at Brady, raising an eyebrow. "And don't tell me you're actually into that kind of thing."

Brady shrugged. "I've tried it before. It's not bad if you season it correctly. Kind of grows on you."

Coop rolled his eyes again, clearly exasperated with both of them. "Good grief. Next thing I know, y'all will be telling me you've gone full vegetarian or vegan. That would be even worse."

Brady clapped Coop on the shoulder. "Don't you worry. I'm not about to give up my burgers anytime soon. Just saying that sometimes a little change isn't the end of the world."

Madeline looked at Coop, then at Brady, and she knew just how much Brady enjoyed getting under Coop's skin a bit.

Coop huffed and stood up with a grumble. "Well, you two can go ahead and try that place if you want, and I'll be sitting right here serving real food to real people," he said, pointing at each of them. "Some things don't need to be fixed. There ain't nothing broken here in Jubilee."

As he stalked off, still muttering under his breath, Madeline finally let out a laugh, nudging Brady with her elbow. "Why do you like riling him up so much?"

Brady smiled. "I can't help it. It's good for him. Keeps him on his toes."

They finished their coffee and slid out of the booth, leaving a tip on the table before making their way to the door. As they stepped outside, Madeline looked across the street at the café, which wasn't open yet but still causing quite a stir.

"You think Coop's ever gonna come around?"

Brady chuckled. "Maybe someday, but I don't think I'd count on it. Some folks just don't like change, and Coop is definitely one of them."

Whitney Cooper walked down Main Street with her arms crossed as she fought back the knot of emotion sitting squarely in the middle of her stomach. It had been a hectic morning at the clinic, and no matter how many times she tried to push her dream out of her head, it always came back when she had a free moment. She had always wanted to open a wellness studio, and it felt like something she was meant to do, but every time she tried to talk to her father about it, his words would echo in her mind: *This town doesn't need some new-age nonsense, Whitney.*

She sighed, thinking about the last time they had spoken about it a couple of weeks ago.

As she got closer to his restaurant, she glanced

toward the café across the street. Workers were hammering away, adjusting the brand-new *Jubilee Vegan Café* sign. The sight of it made her stomach twist into knots. It wasn't because she shared her father's disdain for this new place but because she envied their progress. Someone else was bringing their own vision to life while she was stuck in the same old routine.

She had been working at the clinic as a nurse for five years now. When she wasn't working there, she was helping her dad at his restaurant, something she had done since she was a teenager. It was expected of her. Her father hoped that one day, she would leave the medical world behind and take over the restaurant. If it was up to him, she'd work there all the time.

Most parents would be proud of their children for building a career in the medical field. Even though she wasn't working at a big fancy hospital, she was proud of what she had accomplished. She liked helping people every day. She wanted to do it in her own facility. She wanted to have a place where people could come and do yoga, learn about meditation, get supplements, and basically just take a break from the crazy world. But her father thought all of it was ridiculous. People just needed to pull up their bootstraps and get on with it.

Up ahead, she saw two familiar figures walking out of Coop's Home Cookin'—Brady and Madeline. They always looked so happy, and Whitney had to admit that sometimes she was a little jealous of that. They were both in their fifties and had found love. Here she was in her thirties and couldn't find anyone to share her life with. Of course, her father never approved of anyone, which made things even harder.

Whitney admired Madeline and Brady, especially Madeline, who had had the courage to pursue her dream of becoming an author all those years ago.

"Hey, y'all!" Whitney called, forcing a smile. She wasn't feeling particularly happy this morning.

Brady raised a hand and waved at her. "Well, hey there, Whitney. How's it going?"

She smiled and waved back. "Oh, you know, the usual. Busy at the clinic. I'm sure you've heard that Daddy's grumbling about the café like it's some kind of apocalypse."

Madeline laughed softly. "Yeah, we got an earful about that at breakfast."

"I bet," Whitney said, shaking her head. She hesitated for a moment before asking, "Can I ask y'all something?"

"Of course," Madeline said.

"I've been thinking a lot about opening my own wellness studio here in Jubilee. You know, meditation, yoga, stuff like that. And I really think folks around here would benefit from it. But Daddy, well, you can imagine what he thinks about it."

Brady raised his eyebrows, clearly impressed. "A wellness studio? Whitney, that's a wonderful idea. I'd say the town could use something like that. Everybody's stressed out all the time, no matter where they live."

She felt a flicker of hope, but it dimmed as soon as she thought about her father. "Daddy doesn't see it that way. He says it's a waste of time and that I'd be better off sticking with him at the diner. He thinks the whole idea is a little too modern, that it won't work." She paused, sighing. "And he certainly wouldn't help me fund a place like that. I don't have the money to start a business. I've struggled with my finances my whole life. Daddy has some money set aside for me, but not for something like this."

"I know it's hard to hear from your father that he doesn't believe in your dream because his opinion matters so much to you," Madeline said gently. Whitney nodded. "But," Madeline continued, stepping closer, "if this is something you truly believe in, then you have to try. And I know how scary that can be. When I started writing years ago, people didn't take me seriously at first. Some people in my life even thought it was silly. But I kept going because I

26

couldn't imagine not doing this. And now it's my life. If I hadn't taken that risk, where would I be today?"

Whitney looked at her, taking in her words. She had read some of Madeline's books, and it was hard to believe that she had ever doubted herself.

Brady chimed in, his voice steady. "Your dad's got a strong personality—trust me, I know that. But that doesn't mean he's always right about everything. Sometimes, you have to take a leap and show him you're serious. So if this is what you're passionate about, I'd say go for it."

Whitney felt warmth in her chest. Their words felt like a lifeline.

"Thank you both so much," she said. "It means a lot to hear you say that. I've just been going back and forth in my mind about whether I should bring it up again."

"You do need to bring it up again," Madeline said. "And if you need somebody in your corner, I'm always here."

"Thanks, Madeline. And you too, Brady."

"Anytime," Brady said with a wink.

She gave them a wave as they headed toward Brady's truck, their conversation fading into the air as they walked away.

Whitney stood there with the morning sun

warming her face and let herself feel that sense of hope in her chest. But before she could think about much else, her father poked his head out of the door of the restaurant.

"Come on, Whitney. I've got orders backed up, and I need your help."

W hitney stood behind the counter at Coop's Home Cookin', wiping down the same spot on the counter for the third time in a row. Her father had disappeared somewhere back in the kitchen to check on the latest delivery. He was muttering something about lazy suppliers.

For a moment, the restaurant was pretty quiet, and she was basically alone. Her eyes drifted to the window, where she could see workers carrying boxes and light fixtures inside the Jubilee Vegan Café. The café was so close that it felt like it was taunting her.

For the last several days, she had resisted the temptation to sneak over and take a look. Her father's rants had only grown louder and more persistent. Every time she mentioned the café, he would start into a tirade about how it didn't belong in Jubilee. Honestly, she didn't understand why her father was so threatened by it.

Now, as she stood there looking at the place through the windows, it seemed to be beckoning her on a dare.

She glanced toward the kitchen. She could hear her father's voice barking orders at somebody about a delivery. If she was quick, he might not even notice that she was gone.

Before she could second-guess herself, she untied her apron and folded it neatly on the counter before slipping out the front door. She squinted in the bright sunlight and hurried across the street with her heart thudding in her chest.

She knew she shouldn't do it, but she pushed the door open, and a soft chime announced her arrival.

She paused just inside the doorway, her breath catching. This place was nothing like she'd imagined.

The space was open and airy, with large windows letting in natural light and beautiful views of the mountains beyond. Clean lines and sleek, minimalist décor gave it a welcoming but polished vibe.

Potted plants lined the walls, and warm wooden tables paired with crisp white chairs created a calming atmosphere.

She walked further inside, her fingers brushing the edge of a glossy counter that gleamed under the light. Everything smelled a little bit like citrus or eucalyptus, which was a far cry from the fried smell that she was used to at Coop's.

"Hey there," a deep, friendly voice called out, startling her.

Whitney quickly turned and saw a man walking toward her, wiping his hands on a towel. He was tall and lean, his dark hair slightly messy in a way that made him look like he was completely put together. His shirt sleeves were rolled up, showing off his strong forearms, and he had a warm smile. He wasn't at all what she had expected.

"Oh, hi," she stammered, feeling embarrassed.

"You must be one of Coop's people," he said, his smile widening as he extended his hand. "Tate Morgan. I'm the owner of this little place."

Whitney hesitated for a moment before shaking his hand. She was surprised at his southern accent. She didn't know why. He could have been from anywhere, for all she knew.

"Whitney Cooper," she said. "I just wanted to take a look around. I guess I've been a little curious. My dad owns Coop's."

"Well, I'm glad you stopped by," he said. "Let me show you around. I'm still getting things set up, but I'd love to get your input—hear what you think."

Whitney followed him as he gestured toward the seating area. He talked about the custom-made tables and the local artwork he had put on the walls. He spoke with such easy confidence, clearly passionate about what he was creating there.

"This is more than just a café for me," he said, stopping in front of a row of shelves lined with organic teas and supplements. "I wanted to build a place where people could feel good about what they're putting into their bodies. You know, where you can slow down for a minute and focus on health."

She found herself nodding. "That's exactly what I've been dreaming about," she said without thinking.

He turned to her, his expression curious. "Really?"

"Yeah," she said, feeling a little bit shy. "I've been thinking about opening a wellness studio, you know, a place for yoga, meditation, that sort of thing. My dad, of course, thinks it's a ridiculous idea. He's a little bit old school. He's convinced that Jubilee doesn't need anything like that."

Tate leaned against the counter and crossed his arms as he listened. "You know, people sometimes resist change until they see the benefits for themselves. A wellness studio sounds like the perfect fit for a place like this. Small towns often don't have anywhere to go for holistic healing, and they should have access to those just like the big cities do."

She felt a spark of excitement. "Yeah, that's what I've been saying. I just… I don't know. It's hard to take that first step when the person closest to you doesn't believe in it."

He nodded. "I get that. When I told my family I wanted to leave my corporate job and open this place, well, they thought I'd lost my mind. But I knew it was something I had to do. If you really believe in it, you'll find a way to make it happen—just like I did."

She studied him, surprised by his kindness. She had expected him to be a little more aloof, maybe even condescending. But no, Tate was genuine.

"Thank you," she said. "I didn't expect to hear that today. And I'm sorry for breaking into your place."

He smiled. "Well, just know you've got at least one person in your corner. And for what it's worth, I think your dad will come around eventually. It'll take him a while. I know he probably loves this town with everything he has in him, but he'll see what you're doing is good for everyone."

"I hope you're right," she said, looking toward the door. She knew she couldn't stay there much longer without raising suspicion.

Tate straightened. "Let me know if you ever want to talk about your ideas. I'd love to help however I can, especially since I just opened a business myself."

"Thanks, Tate. I appreciate that, and you have a beautiful place here. I know it's going to do really well."

As she stepped back outside, she had a storm of emotions rolling through her. She couldn't deny that she felt a connection with Tate, even after meeting him just for a few moments. If nothing else, he would be a great friend to her—if her dad wouldn't interfere.

Then she thought about her dad. She could already hear his voice in her head, dismissing everything that Tate stood for and everything she wanted to build.

She looked back at the café one more time before crossing the street. She wanted to spend more time with the man she had just met—the one who understood her— but loyalty was a powerful thing, and as much as she wanted to follow her heart, she just couldn't shake the weight of her father's expectations.

She slipped back into Coop's. Her father barely looked up from his conversation with Wanda, but Whitney's world had shifted in the span of fifteen minutes, and she wasn't sure if things would ever feel the same again.

CHAPTER 3

W hitney adjusted her scrubs and tucked a
stray piece of hair behind her ear as she
hurried down the hallway of the clinic. Her shift had
been a non-stop blur of patients with seasonal aller-
gies, sprained ankles, and even a kid who had stuck a
raisin up his nose. That had been a real adventure. It
was just another busy day in Jubilee, and she hadn't
had a moment to catch her breath.

"Whitney," one of the nurses called from the
front desk. "We've got a walk-in who needs to be
seen. Can you take it?"

She nodded but sighed to herself as she grabbed a
pair of gloves. "Sure thing. What's the issue?"

"Burn on his hand," the nurse said. "He says it's
not too bad, but it is blistered, so we should really
take a look at it."

"Got it," Whitney said, heading toward the small exam room where she sometimes saw patients. Although she wasn't a doctor, as a nurse, she could assess minor injuries and determine the next steps.

She opened the door with her usual professional demeanor but froze when she stepped inside.

Tate Morgan was sitting on the exam table, looking slightly sheepish.

"Oh," she said, blinking in surprise. "It's you."

She glanced down at the iPad in her hand. Of course, she would have known it was him if she had bothered to check the name before walking into the room.

Tate looked up, his mouth curving into a warm smile. "Hey there. Fancy meeting you here."

Whitney's heart fluttered as she stepped further into the room, closing the door behind her. "So, what happened?"

He held up his hand, showing an angry red burn with small blisters forming along his palm. "I was testing out the new oven at the café and forgot to grab a hot pad. So… here I am."

She winced as she rolled the stool over and sat down in front of him. "That looks painful. Let's take care of it."

"Oh, it's not too bad," he said, watching her as she examined his hand. "Honestly, I'm more embarrassed than anything. Rookie mistake. Who forgets a hot pad?"

She couldn't help but smile as she reached for the saline solution and some gauze. "It happens to the best of us. Burns can be tricky, so it's good that you came in."

As she cleaned the wound gently, she became acutely aware of how close they were. She could feel his eyes on her, and it made her flustered in a way she hadn't expected. She barely knew this guy, so why was she having such a strong reaction to him?

"So," Tate said, his voice breaking the silence, "do you always work this hard, or is today just extra busy?"

Whitney looked up at him, smiling slightly. "I'd say this is pretty typical. It's a small clinic, so we get a little bit of everything."

"Well, you're good at it," he said. "I can tell you really care about what you're doing."

Her cheeks warmed at the compliment. She refocused on his hand. "Thank you. I enjoy helping people. It's one of the reasons I want to open a wellness studio."

"You're serious about that, huh?"

"I am," she said, her voice softening. "I've been dreaming about it for years, but it's hard to take that first step, especially when my own father thinks it's a stupid idea."

He didn't respond immediately, but when she looked up at him, his expression softened. "You know, sometimes the people who love us the most have the hardest time seeing us take big risks. But that doesn't mean they don't want us to succeed."

Her hands paused for a moment as she worked. Hearing that from him felt different—like he actually understood her.

"Maybe," she said quietly, returning to work on his hand. "But it's still hard to feel like he doesn't believe in me."

Tate nodded. "I get that. I really do."

The room was silent for a moment except for the faint hum of clinic noises in the background. She finished cleaning the burn and applied a soothing ointment.

"Again, you're really good at this," he said after a while. "I mean it—you've got a way of making people feel cared for."

When she looked up and met his eyes, there was something in his expression that made her heart skip—a warmth and openness she hadn't seen in a man before.

"Thank you," she said, suddenly feeling very shy. She wrapped his hand with clean gauze and secured it. "Okay, that should do it. Keep it clean and dry for the next few days, and don't pop any of the blisters. If it gets worse or doesn't heal, come back and see us."

"Yes, ma'am," he said with a small grin.

She laughed and stood, tossing her gloves into the trash. "I'm serious, Tate. Take care of it. Don't be a guy about it."

"I will," he said, sliding off the exam table. "And thanks, Whitney."

She looked at him, feeling a strange connection. "Anytime."

He smiled and started toward the door, but just before he stepped out, he turned back. "You know, that wellness studio of yours—it's going to happen. I can see it. You've got too much passion for it not to."

"Thanks, Tate. I hope you're right."

With that, he was gone, leaving her standing in the empty room with her heart racing and her mind spinning.

She leaned against the counter, taking a deep breath to steady herself. Tate Morgan was unlike anyone she'd ever met—genuine, kind, and somehow able to understand her in a way that few people ever had.

But as much as she wanted to hold on to the warmth of that moment, the nagging voice in the back of her mind—her father's voice—warned her to be cautious.

"Hey, Whitney!" the nurse called from the hallway.

"Yeah?" she responded, snapping out of her thoughts.

"We've got a little boy out here who stuck a bead up his nose."

Whitney shook her head and smiled faintly as she grabbed a fresh pair of gloves. "On my way."

Whitney stood behind the counter at Coop's Home Cookin', refilling salt shakers and wiping down menus, but her heart just wasn't in it. Her eyes kept drifting toward the window, where she could see Tate's place across the street. The sleek new sign gleamed in the sunlight, and through the window, she caught faint glimpses of movement as people came and went now that the café had officially opened for business.

Her father's voice snapped her out of her thoughts. "Whitney, are you listening to me?"

She turned, blinking as if she'd been caught sneaking a cookie before dinner. "Oh… yeah, sorry. What was that?"

Coop frowned, wiping his hands on a dish towel as he exited the kitchen. "I said table four needs coffee, and I'm almost out of biscuits back here."

"Oh, right. I'll get the coffee," she said, grabbing the pot and heading toward the table.

When she returned to the counter, she tried to focus, folding napkins into neat little triangles and arranging them in holders. But her gaze kept slipping back to the café, drawn to its modern charm and the steady stream of customers.

"Whitney?" Coop said sharply, his tone carrying a note of suspicion.

She jumped and turned to face him. "What?" she asked, placing a hand on her chest.

"You keep staring out that window," he said, his eyes narrowing. "What's got you so distracted today?"

"Nothing," she said quickly. "I'm just tired, that's all."

He didn't look convinced. "You're not tired. You're distracted. And I bet I know what's got your attention." He pointed his thumb toward the window. "That ridiculous café. Let me guess, you're worried it's gonna hurt our business, aren't you?"

She sighed, hoping a little white lie might satisfy him. "Something like that."

"Well, don't you be worried," he said gruffly,

tossing the dish towel over his shoulder. "It's a waste of time, that's what it is. Ain't nobody around here going to trade in good ol' home cooking for over-priced rabbit food. You mark my words; they'll be closed in six months."

Whitney pressed her lips together, biting back a reply. Her father wouldn't change his mind about the café anytime soon, and arguing would only make things worse.

As Coop launched into another rant about small-town traditions and the absurdity of fancy big-city ideas, she caught a glimpse of someone walking across the street, heading straight for Coop's.

It was Tate.

Her heart skipped a beat as she watched him approach, a small bag in his hand. He was almost at the door when panic set in.

"I'll be right back," she said quickly, cutting her father off mid-rant.

"What? Where are you going?" he demanded.

"I forgot something in my car," she called over her shoulder, already heading toward the door.

She stepped outside, squinting in the sunlight, and quickly waved to get Tate's attention. He stopped mid-step, his brow furrowing in confusion as she gestured for him to move away from the windows. He followed her around the side of the building, out of Coop's line of sight.

"Everything okay?" he asked.

"Yeah, fine," she said, out of breath, glancing over her shoulder to make sure they weren't being watched. "My dad… well, let's just say I don't think he'd be too welcoming to you today. He's kind of in a mood."

Tate smiled, holding up the bag. "I just wanted to give you this—a little thank you for helping me with my hand."

She took the bag and peeked inside, finding a neatly wrapped container with what looked like freshly baked muffins. She smiled. "This is very sweet of you. Thank you. How's the hand healing?"

"Well, I guess you'd have to tell me," he said, holding out his bandaged hand.

She set the bag aside on the trunk of her car and gestured for him to extend his hand. He did, and she carefully unwrapped the gauze, her fingers brushing against his skin as she worked.

His palm was still red, but the blisters had begun to shrink, and the wound looked clean and healthy.

"Not too bad," she said. "You've been taking good care of it."

"Following doctor's orders," he teased.

"Well, I'm not a doctor," she said, laughing softly

as she rewrapped his hand. "But you're a good patient. Just keep it clean and dry, and you'll be good as new in no time."

"Thank you," he said, his gaze lingering for a moment.

The air between them shifted, and Whitney's hand froze as she finished securing the bandage. When she looked up, her breath caught at the warmth in his eyes. For a moment, it felt like the whole world had fallen away, leaving just the two of them standing in the parking lot with the Blue Ridge Mountains as their backdrop.

"You're very good at this," he said, his voice softer now.

"It's my job," she said, laughing nervously.

"No, it's more than that. You care. That's rare in this world."

Her heart thudded as she quickly stepped back. "I should get back inside," she said, glancing toward the diner. "I don't want my daddy coming out here and making a big scene."

Tate nodded. "Thanks again, Whitney. For everything."

She watched as he turned and walked back across the street, disappearing into the café.

Her fingers brushed over the bag he had given her. She quickly put it in her car. Taking a deep breath, she slipped back inside. Coop was still ranting to Wanda about the café and didn't even glance her way as she returned to the counter.

But Whitney's world felt different now. Tate Morgan had gotten under her skin, and no matter how hard she tried, she wasn't sure she'd ever be able to keep her distance.

Madeline sat at her small writing desk, her fingers hovering over the keyboard. Outside the window, the Blue Ridge Mountains stretched across the horizon like a living postcard. Morning mist curled through the trees, and sunlight peeked through the clouds. This view always made her stop and stare, reminding her why she had chosen to settle in Jubilee.

But today, it wasn't enough to clear her mind. She stared at the blinking cursor on her screen, the words she'd already written feeling flat and uninspired. The looming deadline for her new book pressed silently in the back of her mind, a weight she couldn't shake.

"Come on, Madeline," she muttered to herself. "You've done this a million times before. Just start."

Her hands moved to type a new sentence, but nothing came.

A knock on the door interrupted her thoughts, offering the perfect excuse to stop writing for a few minutes.

"Hey, sweetheart," came Brady's familiar drawl as he stepped inside, holding a steaming cup of coffee. "Figured you could use this little pick-me-up."

She turned in her chair, a smile spreading across her face. "Oh my gosh, you're a lifesaver," she said, reaching for the cup. "How did you know I was struggling?"

He shrugged, leaning casually against the doorframe. "You always get that furrowed look on your face when you're stuck. Plus, it's a safe bet. You're always happy to see coffee no matter what."

She laughed and took a sip, savoring the rich, slightly sweet brew. "You're not wrong. Where'd you get this?"

"Coop's," he said, stepping further into the room. "Perky's was too packed this morning, and when I walked into Coop's, Wanda practically shoved it in my hands. Said you'd appreciate it more than I would."

"Well, she's right about that," Madeline said with a chuckle. "Tell her I owe her one."

He pulled up a chair and settled across from her,

his own coffee in hand. For a while, they sat in comfortable silence. The only sounds were the tapping of her keyboard and the occasional chirping of birds outside.

As the morning stretched on, Madeline stole a glance at him. He was scrolling through his phone, concentrating on whatever he was reading. She admired the quiet strength of his features, the way his jawline tensed when he was focused, and the little crinkles at the corners of his eyes when he smiled.

"What are you working on over there?" she asked, leaning back in her chair and stretching.

"Oh, just some stuff for the farm," he said. "You know, Gilbert's been gnawing on the fence again, so I'm trying to figure out how to keep that little booger from destroying it completely."

She laughed softly. "That goat has more personality than most people I know."

"Yeah, tell me about it," he said, shaking his head. "I think he's doing it just to mess with me at this point," he said, laughing. "You know," he added after a moment, "you look pretty good when you're working. All focused and determined."

She felt a blush creep up her neck. "Is that your way of saying I look like a stressed-out mess?"

"No, not at all," he said. "It's just nice to see you in

your element. You've got this whole creative energy thing going on. It's kind of cool."

She rolled her eyes. "Flattery will get you nowhere, Brady Nolan."

"Are you sure about that?" he asked with a wink, reaching across the desk to rub his thumb against the top of her hand.

She shook her head and turned back to her computer. She wasn't going to let him distract her today. She had too much to do.

Hours passed in a peaceful rhythm as he worked on his phone, occasionally muttering about farm supplies or typing out a text, while Madeline lost herself in the world of her story. Finally, she found her groove, the words flowing more quickly than they had all morning.

Every now and then, they exchanged a glance or a smile. At one point, Brady got up to stretch and walked over to the window.

"You've got the best view in town. You know that?"

"Yes, I'm aware," Madeline said, looking up from her screen. "It's part of the reason I decided to stay here."

"Well, the view's nice," he said, turning back to her. "But I'd argue it's not the best thing about this house."

She raised an eyebrow. "Oh? And what is?"

He leaned against the window frame. "You."

Her breath caught for a moment. She opened her mouth to reply, but before she could, a loud knock echoed through the house.

"Madeline! Brady! Are y'all in there?"

She laughed softly, recognizing the voice immediately. She stood and opened the front door to find Geneva standing on the porch, her hands on her hips. She was dressed in her usual hiking boots and cargo pants, her gray hair pulled into a messy ponytail. A bundle of herbs stuck out of the pocket of her jacket, and a pair of heavy gloves dangled from one hand.

"Morning, Geneva," Madeline said, stepping aside to let her in.

"Morning," Geneva said, breezing past her. She spotted Brady and smiled. "Just the man I need to see."

Brady raised an eyebrow. "What's going on now, Geneva?"

"Well," she began, placing her gloves on the table, "I've got a tree leaning dangerously close to my cabin, and I figured I'd better do something about it before it decides to crash through my roof. I'd handle it myself, but I'm not as spry as I used to be. Think you could help me out with the chainsaw?"

He chuckled. "Geneva, you've been handling that chainsaw longer than I've been alive. You sure you need me?"

"Don't you sass me, boy," Geneva said, wagging her finger at him. "I just need an extra set of hands to make sure I don't take out my whole porch in the process."

He stood and grabbed his jacket. "Okay, okay, let's go save your house."

Geneva smiled and turned to Madeline. "You can come too if you want. Maybe bring that camera of yours. We'll get a good shot of Brady working for once."

Madeline laughed. "I think I'll stay here and keep writing. But please make sure he doesn't hurt himself, okay?"

Geneva winked. "No promises."

CHAPTER 4

W hitney opened the door to Perky's Coffee Shop and inhaled the comforting scent of roasted coffee beans and fresh-baked pastries that lined the glass cases. Just looking at them made her gain weight. The shop was bustling with the usual afternoon crowd, a mix of locals catching up on gossip and tourists soaking in the charm of Jubilee.

She had just finished another long shift at the clinic. Her scrubs felt heavy on her shoulders, and exhaustion weighed her down. Her father had called earlier, asking if she could come help at the restaurant, but for once, she told him no. She just wasn't up for more chaos today. She didn't want to hear him complaining about the new vegan café, and she definitely didn't want to hear him telling her that her dreams were silly.

She needed a moment to herself, and Perky's was the perfect refuge.

Walking up to the counter, she ordered her usual caramel latte, her eyes drifting as she waited. That's when she spotted a familiar figure sitting by the window. Madeline was hunched over her laptop, a steaming mug of coffee beside her and a look of frustration etched on her face.

Whitney smiled and waved. Latte in hand, she made her way across the room and tapped on Madeline's table.

"Mind if I join you?"

Madeline looked up, her expression softening into a smile. "Of course, Whitney, sit down. You actually just saved me from another hour of staring at a blank screen."

Whitney laughed as she slid into the chair across from her. "Writer's block?"

"The worst case I've had in a long time," Madeline admitted, shutting her laptop with a sigh. "I thought maybe a change in scenery would help, but so far, all I've managed to do is drink way too much coffee."

"Well, I'm glad I'm not the only one sneaking away from responsibilities today," Whitney said. She took a sip of her latte, savoring the warm, sweet flavor.

Madeline raised an eyebrow. "Sneaking away?"

Whitney leaned back in her chair. "Dad wanted me to help at the diner after my shift, but I told him I was too tired. It's not exactly a lie—I'm exhausted, mentally and physically—but I just needed a break, you know?"

Madeline nodded. "Sometimes you have to put yourself first. Your dad's going to survive without you for one night."

"Yeah, tell him that," Whitney said with a small smile. She took another sip of her latte, then asked, "Anyway, how's your mom? I haven't seen her around town lately."

Madeline chuckled. "Oh, she and Burt decided to take a little trip to Pigeon Forge. They're seeing the shows and probably eating their weight in pancakes. I'm sure she'll return with a million stories to tell."

Whitney laughed. "That sounds like your mom. Did Jasmine and Anna go with them? I thought I heard something about a family trip."

"They did," Madeline confirmed, referring to Brady's sister and niece who lived with him. "The two of them tagged along. It's good for them to get out of town for a bit. Brady and I were invited, but we decided to stay back. Too much going on around here, and I figured I'd use the quiet time to get some writing done—or so I thought," she said, gesturing to her laptop.

"Well, at least you're trying."

They laughed, and Whitney felt some of the tension in her shoulders ease. She took another sip of her latte, hesitating momentarily before speaking again.

"Can I tell you something?" she asked softly.

"Of course," Madeline said, leaning in slightly.

Whitney looked down at her cup, swirling the foam with her straw. "Well, I've been thinking a lot about Tate—the guy who owns the vegan restaurant."

Madeline tilted her head. "Oh, you've met him?"

Whitney nodded, feeling a blush rise to her cheeks. "Yes, I snuck over to the café one day out of curiosity. Just wanted to take a look. He was there. He's nothing like I thought he'd be—very nice, kind, cordial. Then, a few days later, he came to the clinic because he burned his hand, and I was the one to take care of it."

Madeline's lips curved into a knowing smile, and Whitney sighed.

"I don't know. He's just different. He's so nice, and he really seems to get me. We're very much alike. We talked about wellness and community and everything I've been dreaming about for years. It's like he understood without me having to explain everything. It's been a long time since I connected with somebody like that."

"Sounds like he made quite the impression," Madeline said.

"He did," Whitney admitted, smiling. "But it's not just that. It's like he sees the things I want to do and the person I want to be, and he doesn't think it's silly. He doesn't think it's impossible. He believes in it."

"Whitney, that's a rare thing. You deserve someone in your life who sees you for who you are and supports your dreams—whether it's friendship or something more. It sounds like Tate could be that for you, just like Brady is for me."

"Maybe," Whitney said with a sigh. "But what about my dad? He'd lose his mind if he knew I was spending any time with Tate, let alone considering him a friend. It feels impossible to balance my loyalty to my dad with everything I want for myself."

Madeline reached across the table and squeezed Whitney's hand. "I know it's hard, but at the end of the day, this is your life—not your dad's. If you follow your heart, it doesn't mean you're betraying him. It means you're being true to yourself. He's had his chance to live his own life, and you should have your chance to live yours."

Whitney nodded slowly. "I guess I just don't know if I'm brave enough."

"You are," Madeline said firmly. "I've seen it. You're very strong, Whitney, and when the time comes, you're going to make the right choice for you."

"Thanks, Madeline. I needed to hear that."

"Anytime," Madeline said, smiling warmly. "Now, what do you say we order a couple of pastries and avoid all our responsibilities for at least another hour?"

Whitney laughed, nodding. "I'd say that sounds perfect."

Madeline set the last dish on the table. They were having a steaming pot of chicken and dumplings. The aroma filled the kitchen, mingling with the scent of the biscuits that she'd baked earlier. Brady was already seated at the table, pouring a glass of sweet tea for each of them.

"This looks great, Madeline," he said. "You've outdone yourself yet again. You've become quite the Southern chef. Maybe you could write a cookbook one day."

She laughed softly, sitting down across from him.

"Well, I've been working very hard on my Southern cooking skills since I moved to Jubilee, and I figured since it's Sunday, we could use a proper dinner for a change."

He lifted his glass as a mock toast. "To proper dinners and good company."

She rolled her eyes and smiled as they dug into the food. As usual, the conversation flowed easily. Brady discussed Gilbert's latest antics, updated her about the farm, and discussed her struggles with her newest book.

Just as they were settling into a comfortable rhythm, Brady's phone buzzed on the table, a distinct tone signaling a call-out. His hand stilled as he was reaching for a biscuit, and he let out a quiet sigh.

"Duty calls," he said, pushing back from his chair and standing.

Madeline frowned, watching as he grabbed his keys from the counter. "What is it?"

"Just a small fire," he said. "Probably nothing, just routine."

She followed him to the doorway, leaning against the frame as he slipped on his boots. "Please be careful," she said, trying to keep the worry out of her voice.

He paused, turning back to her with a reassuring

smile. "I'm always careful. I'll be back before you know it."

Brady had been on the volunteer fire department for many years, even before he met Madeline, but since she had met him, he hadn't had to go out on many calls until recently. He gave her a quick kiss on the lips, and with that, he was gone, the sound of his truck rumbling down the dirt road into the quiet of the evening.

She stood there for a moment, hugging herself, staring out at the empty spot where his truck had been. She hated this feeling, this nagging worry that crept up from her stomach to her chest every time he had to go on one of these calls. They hadn't happened often, but this unusually dry season had made the fires more frequent, and she just couldn't shake the fear that one day, something wasn't going to go as planned. There had been so many big fires in the adjoining towns over the years that she had heard about. Some had been devastating. Some had taken lives.

She closed the door and returned to the kitchen, where a half-eaten meal sat on the table, a reminder of his absence. She cleared the plates and wrapped up the leftovers, trying to distract herself by tidying up. Once the kitchen was clean, she went to her writing desk and opened her laptop, determined to at least focus on her next book. But minutes turned into hours, and her mind kept drifting back to Brady.

She imagined him out there, in all of his gear, surrounded by heat and smoke, trying to keep the town safe. She pictured his steady hands and his calm demeanor, the qualities that made him so good at what he did, but those same qualities were what made it so hard for her to say how much she worried about him. She couldn't ask him to ever give up that job. Being a firefighter was part of who he was, part of the sense of duty to the community that he loved, and she loved that about him, even if it meant that she had to live with this low-level, constant anxiety that came with it when he was on a call.

Suddenly, the sound of tires crunching on the gravel outside broke her train of thought. She jumped up from her desk and ran to the window, relief washing over her when she saw Brady's truck pulling into the driveway.

A few moments later, the front door opened, and he stepped inside. "Hey," he said, his voice steady as always.

Madeline ran across the room, wrapping her arms around him before she could think twice. "You're okay," she said, her face pressed into the side of his neck.

He laughed, his arms wrapping around her. "I told you it was routine, nothing to worry about."

She pulled back with her hands resting on his shoulders. "You smell like smoke."

"Well, it was a *fire*," he said with a grin.

Madeline swatted at his arm. "You're impossible, you know that?"

"Yeah, but you like me anyway," he teased as he kissed her forehead.

As much as she wanted to scold him for not understanding her worry, she knew it wouldn't do any good. This is who he was: steady, dependable, and completely devoted to helping others.

"I saved you some dinner," she said, pulling his hand toward the kitchen. "Figured you'd be hungry when you got back."

"You're the best," he said.

Coop sat at the corner booth in his diner, his face frowning as he reviewed the day's receipts. His usually busy restaurant was quiet now, the kitchen's hum reduced to just the occasional clang of a pot or pan as Wanda cleaned up for the evening. He tapped his favorite pen against the table, his jaw clenching tightly.

"Another slow day," he muttered under his breath, shaking his head.

Whitney walked over cautiously, carrying a tray of clean salt shakers to restock the tables. She didn't even need to ask what was bothering him. His expression said it all.

"Everything all right, Daddy?" she asked, setting the tray down and slipping into the seat across from him.

"No, it's not," he snapped, tossing the pen onto the table. "Look at this." He gestured to a stack of receipts. "Sales are down again this week. We're bleeding money here, Whitney."

She looked at the receipts, trying to figure out the best way to respond. "Well, it's been a little slow, but it happens sometimes, Daddy. Remember last summer when—"

"Don't give me that," he interrupted. "This isn't just a slow spell, and you know it. It's that fancy cafe across the street. They're stealing my customers, plain and simple."

Whitney tried to keep her tone neutral. "Daddy, we've had ups and downs before. This could be the very same thing. It might not have anything to do with that cafe. All your regulars are still here every day."

"Not about the cafe," he scoffed, leaning back

against the booth. "Well, what else could it be? Ever since they opened, people have been going over there for their overpriced smoothies and salads instead of coming here to eat real food, good food. I see them walk right past my door with those little paper cup samples."

"People like trying new things," Whitney said. "It doesn't mean they won't come back here. Coop's has been a staple in Jubilee for over forty years. They're not going to forget that."

"Staple or not, it doesn't matter if I can't pay the bills. We'll have to close the doors. And what really gets me is that guy, that Tate Morgan, thinking he can just waltz into town and take over like he's God's gift to Jubilee."

Whitney stiffened at the mention of Tate's name. She somehow felt protective of him. She kept her gaze on the table, hoping her father wouldn't notice the flush creeping up her neck.

"Daddy," she said gently, "maybe it's not at all about competition. People like variety. They may go there one day and come here the next. That's not necessarily a bad thing."

He narrowed his eyes at her. "You sound like you're defending him."

"Well, I'm not," Whitney said quickly. "I'm just saying that we don't know for sure that the cafe is the reason sales were down today. It could be anything. The economy, the season, people traveling."

"Don't give me excuses, Whitney. I know what I see. I've been running this business for decades, and I know what my numbers should be. That place is a problem, and the sooner people realize it, the better."

She wanted to tell him the truth—that she'd met Tate, that she'd been to the restaurant, that she'd treated him at the clinic—but she knew exactly how he would react, and she still couldn't bear the thought of disappointing him. When her mother died when Whitney was in elementary school, the only person she had in the world was her father. No other family, no siblings. He was her world, and she just did not want to upset him.

"You're awfully quiet. Something you're not telling me?"

Whitney's heart raced. "No, Daddy. I'm just tired, that's all."

"You need to remember where your loyalties lie, Whitney Faith. Family comes first, always."

The words stung more than she expected. She nodded and rose from the table. "I know, Daddy. I need to get back to work."

He didn't stop her as she walked away, but she could feel his frustration hanging heavy in the air, following her like a shadow. She'd never seen her father act like this—well, at least not for this long. He often ranted and vented about every little thing, but this seemed to really be weighing heavily on him, and she worried about him, worried about his health.

She stepped into the kitchen, her hands shaking as she grabbed a dish towel and started wiping down the counters. She was torn, caught between her father's unrealistic expectations and the new connection she felt with Tate. Tate, the man who understood her dreams in a way her father never could.

CHAPTER 5

Whitney stood on the sidewalk outside of Jubilee Vegan Cafe, her heart beating faster than she wanted to admit. She looked over her shoulder, expecting her father to come storming across the street and drag her back to the diner, but nobody was watching. She took a deep breath and opened the door.

The soft chime of the bell greeted her, followed by a warm cinnamon scent she remembered from her first visit. The cafe was busy, with tables filled with locals and tourists, conversations and clinking utensils filling the air. She looked across the room, her eyes immediately landing on Tate. He stood behind the counter, chatting with a customer as he handed them a steaming bowl of soup. His smile was easy, his movements confident, and Whitney couldn't help but admire the way he seemed to be completely at home here.

She stood near the door, not wanting to interrupt, but Tate spotted her almost instantly. His face seemed to light up, and he raised his hand to wave her over. She felt a mix of guilt and excitement, but the warmth of his smile eased her nerves, and she walked toward him.

"Whitney," he said, stepping out from behind the counter. "I was hoping I would see you again."

"Hey," she said, tucking a strand of hair behind her ear. "I don't want to interrupt. I just thought I'd stop by."

"Well, I'm sure glad you did," he said. "How about you sit down for a minute? I was going to take a break anyway."

Before she could argue, he took her to a cozy table near the window and pointed for her to sit. A few moments later, he came back with two bowls of black bean soup and slices of cornbread on small plates.

"This is one of my favorites. It's our special today," he said, sliding a bowl in front of her. "Black bean soup and plant-based oil-free cornbread. Trust me, it's a lot better than it sounds."

She smiled as she picked up her spoon, the rich

aroma of the soup making her mouth water. "I'll take your word for it."

She took a bite and found the flavors warm and comforting with just the right amount of spice. The cornbread was actually very moist and flavorful.

"This is actually very good," she said. "I wasn't expecting it to be this good."

"See, healthy food doesn't have to be boring," he said, laughing.

As they ate, he leaned back in his chair. "You know, I started this place because of my grandmother."

"Your grandmother?"

"Yeah," he said. "She had diabetes, and it really affected her quality of life. I loved her a lot, and watching her struggle was very difficult. Made me realize how important it is to take care of your body, and food plays such a big role in that. So I got into healthy eating and decided I wanted to help other people too."

"That's really amazing, Tate. You're doing something important here."

"Thank you," he said. "But you know, it's not about the food completely. It's about creating a space where people feel welcome. I want people to come and slow down for a bit, kind of like what you were saying about your wellness studio. That's why I know you should go for it."

She stared down at her bowl. "It's just complicated. I told you my dad won't support it, and I don't have the resources to make that happen on my own."

He leaned forward, his eyes meeting hers. "Whitney, you can't let other people's doubts stop you from chasing your dreams. They had their chance to chase their dreams, and you deserve the same. If it's what you want, you'll find a way, and if you need help figuring out the logistics, I just opened a business. I'd be happy to sit down with you and work on a business plan."

"You'd do that?"

"Of course," he said without hesitation. "I've been where you are. I know just how overwhelming all of this can feel. You don't have to do it all alone."

She smiled for the first time in a long time. She found someone who truly understood her. "Thank you," she said softly.

He waved his hand. "Don't thank me yet. How about we meet at Perky's tomorrow and start brainstorming? My manager will have things covered here, so I'm free. You want to say around ten?"

She nodded. "I'm off from the clinic tomorrow, so that sounds perfect."

As they finished their meal and said goodbye,

Whitney felt a strange mix of emotions swirling in her gut. Guilt for sneaking away and talking to him, but also a sense of hope she hadn't felt in years. Tate believed in her, and for the first time, she had started to believe in herself, too.

Brady leaned against the old fence post, watching as Gilbert, his constantly mischievous goat, chewed contentedly on a patch of grass. The late afternoon sun cast a warm glow over the farm, the fields stretching out in every direction. The beauty of the land never failed to amaze him. He wondered how other people got by without witnessing something like this every single day.

Today, the setting seemed perfect for some downtime, and Brady hoped Coop might appreciate the peaceful surroundings, even if just for a little while. Coop, whom he had invited over for the day, stood a few feet away, his hands stuffed in his pockets, staring at the newly rebuilt barn.

"Well, you've done a nice job out here, Brady," Coop said, his tone softer than usual. "Looks good."

"Thanks," Brady replied, pointing toward the house in the distance. "You want to see the house next? We totally changed the layout when we rebuilt it after the fire."

Coop nodded, following Brady across the gravel driveway. "I can't imagine what it was like to lose everything in that fire," he said quietly. "Must've felt like the end of the world."

"I won't lie, it was tough," Brady said, opening the back door to the house. "But, you know, it gave me a chance to rethink some things and make improvements I'd been putting off for years."

Inside, the house smelled like fresh wood and new paint. Brady led Coop through the kitchen, pointing out the new cabinets and updated appliances, and then into the living room, where large windows framed a stunning view of the mountains.

Coop let out a low whistle. "Man, that's a view you've got here. Makes me wonder why I spend most of my life stuck behind a counter."

Brady laughed. "Well, it's not too late to start enjoying life, Coop. Plus, you can see the mountains out of the diner windows, too. You could take a day or two off every now and then. Come up here, ride some horses."

Coop shook his head. "Nah, I wouldn't know what to do with myself if I took time off. Besides, the diner needs me. Always has, always will."

"Maybe so," Brady said as they stepped back

outside. "But it's good to take a break every now and then. Clears your head."

They walked into the barn, its doors creaking as Brady pushed them open. "I got the roof reinforced and added more storage," Brady said, pointing toward the loft. "Should be set for the next twenty years, at least."

Coop nodded, running his hand along a polished wooden beam. "It's solid. You've got yourself a nice setup here, Brady."

"Thanks," he said, leaning against a stack of hay bales. "So, you ever think about changing things up at the diner? Trying some new stuff?"

Coop's head snapped toward him, his eyebrow furrowing. "What in the holy heck is that supposed to mean?"

"I'm just saying," Brady continued carefully, "maybe you could bring in some new ideas without changing what makes Coop's special. Like, maybe you could collaborate with that new guy on something."

Coop's expression darkened, and he crossed his arms over his broad chest. "Tate? You mean the vegan guy? He's the reason my sales are down. Why in the world would I want to work with him?"

Brady sighed, rubbing the back of his neck. "Coop, I get it. Change is hard, but Jubilee's gonna grow whether we like it or not. People are looking for variety. Maybe instead of fighting it, you could find a way to adapt."

"Adapt?" Coop scoffed. "Why do I have to change? My diner's been here for over forty years. People know exactly what to expect when they walk through those doors, and that's what keeps them coming back."

"Is it, though?" Brady asked gently. "Or is it because people know you? Because they feel like they're with family when they're in your place. That's what really matters. The food is just a little part of it."

Coop shook his head. "That's easy for you to say, Brady. You're not the one watching your longtime customers walk right past your door to go to some vegan place."

"I just think you've got to offer more than biscuits and gravy, Coop. I'm not talking about food. People love you, man. They'd follow your lead if you decided to try something different."

Coop's jaw tightened. "And now Whitney's talking about starting some silly wellness studio."

"Well, what's wrong with that?"

"What's wrong with that?" Coop repeated. "This town doesn't need all this new-age nonsense. It's all a waste of time, and she's better off sticking with the diner or her job as a nurse. Those are the places where she belongs."

"Let me ask you something. When you started your diner years ago, did anyone tell you it was a waste of time?"

Coop hesitated, his shoulders stiffening.

"I bet they did," Brady said, "and you didn't listen, did you? You followed your dream, and look what you've built for yourself. Don't you think your daughter deserves the same chance?"

"That's different," Coop grumbled. "She's got a good job at that clinic. She doesn't need to chase some pipe dream."

"Well, maybe it's not a pipe dream. Maybe it's her dream. If anyone should understand that, it's you."

Coop stared at the barn floor, the silence stretching between them. Finally, he sighed. "I don't know, Brady. I just… I don't want to see her get hurt."

Brady placed a hand on Coop's shoulder, his grip firm. "I understand, but sometimes you have to let her try, even if she fails. That's the best way to show her you believe in her. She's got something special. Don't hold her back because you're afraid."

"I'll think about it," Coop said gruffly.

"That's all I'm asking," Brady said. "Now, how

about we go check on Gilbert? He's probably gnawing on something he shouldn't be."

Whitney pulled nervously at the hem of her red cardigan as she walked into Perky's Coffee Shop. The shop was buzzing with the usual mix of tourists and locals, and the warm scent of coffee mingled with a faint smell of pastries. She looked around the room, her stomach nervously flipping when she finally spotted Tate at a corner table with a notebook and a laptop in front of him. He caught her eye and smiled, standing and waving at her.

Taking a deep breath, she made her way to the table.

"Hey," she said, sliding into the seat across from him.

"Hey," he said, his smile widening. "Glad you could make it. I got us a couple of coffees. Hope you like a caramel latte. If not, I can go get you something else."

"I love caramel lattes! They're actually my favorite drink here," she said, wrapping her hands around the warm cup. "Thanks." She wondered how he knew that about her. Maybe there was a connection there, or maybe she was being silly, and it was just a safe bet that a woman would like a sweet drink.

"No problem," he said, flipping the notebook open in front of him. "So, business plans. I figured we'd start with the basics—your goals, your vision, what you want your studio to be. Does that sound okay?"

She nodded, her nerves starting to ease slightly. "That sounds great. I've never even talked about it in detail with anyone, so I'm not completely sure where to start."

"Well, we'll take it step by step," he said, pulling a pen from his pocket. "So, the first question is, why do you want to open a wellness studio?"

She thought for a moment, trying to put her feelings into words. "I've always wanted to help people. I love working at the clinic, but I want to do more than just treat symptoms after somebody is already sick. I want to create a space where people can get better—or can prevent disease altogether—using mind, body, and spirit. A place where they can come, slow down, and learn to take care of themselves."

His pen moved quickly across the page as he focused entirely on her words. "Love that," he said. "And what kind of services would you offer? Yoga, meditation, but what else?"

RACHEL HANNA

"Maybe nutrition workshops or mindfulness classes. I would even be open to herbal remedies or aromatherapy," she said, feeling her excitement grow as she spoke. "I want it to be a one-stop shop for wellness. I want people to come from all around to visit Jubilee just to come to my place."

He nodded as he jotted notes. "Okay, and who's your target audience? Locals? Tourists? Both?"

"Both," Whitney said quickly. "I think there's such a potential to draw in visitors, but I also want it to be a great space for the community."

"Good," he said, his voice encouraging. "You're already thinking about your market, and that's a great start."

As they continued talking and Tate asked more questions about pricing, location, and potential obstacles, she found herself opening up more than she ever had about her dream. At one point, she reached for the pen he was holding to make a note in his notebook, and their hands brushed. The contact was brief, but she felt a jolt go through her like nothing she'd ever felt before. She quickly pulled her hand back, looking up to see if he'd noticed.

He was looking at her, his expression soft. "Sorry," he said. "I didn't mean to startle you."

"Oh, it's fine," she said. "I shouldn't have reached for it while you were writing."

He smiled, and for a moment, the air between them felt electrically charged, as if the world around them had disappeared and it was just the two of them. Clearing his throat, he leaned back.

"So, let's talk numbers. Do you have any savings or money to put toward this? Are you looking for investors?"

She sighed. "That's the tricky part. I don't have much saved, and my dad definitely is not going to help. He doesn't believe in the idea, so why would he put money toward it?"

"It is tough, but there are options. Small business loans, grants for women entrepreneurs—there's a lot out there if you know where to look."

"Do you think I could qualify for something like that?"

"Sure," Tate said. "You've got a great vision, and once we get this plan written out, you'll have the foundation you need to go pitch it. I'll help you with the research, and I can even connect you with some people I know who helped me."

"Really?" she asked.

"Of course," he said without hesitation. "I believe in what you're trying to do, Whitney, and I know you can make it happen. And maybe once you have your studio, we can work together on some things."

She smiled, the warmth of his words wrapping

around her like a blanket. For the first time, this dream didn't seem like such a fantasy. It was something real and possibly achievable.

They leaned over the notebook together, brainstorming ideas for marketing and budgeting, and their heads came so close that she could feel the warmth coming off of him. At one point, they both reached for the same page, their shoulders brushing.

"Sorry," Tate said.

"It's okay."

Their eyes met, and just for a moment, she felt the world tilt slightly. She could feel the weight of his gaze and the unspoken connection growing between them. But before she could process any other feelings, he cleared his throat and leaned back.

"We're making great progress."

"Yeah," Whitney said, quieter than she'd intended. "We are."

When they wrapped up their meeting with a promise to follow up soon, Whitney left the cafe. She glanced back at Tate. He was still sitting at the table, watching her with a smile. She walked outside onto the sidewalk, wishing she could have spent the day sitting there with him, talking about her dreams. She was closer than ever to making them a reality.

CHAPTER 6

Whitney pushed open the glass door of Away With Words, hearing the jingle of a bell above her head as she walked into the cozy bookstore. It always smelled like paper and vanilla because Clemmy kept the best candles lit. It was immediately a soothing balm to the tension that she had carried all day. She hadn't been to the bookstore in a long time. Life at the clinic and the diner didn't leave her a lot of time for leisure, but today, she needed more than just coffee and fresh air. She needed guidance.

"Well, Whitney Cooper, is that you?" Clemmy's cheerful voice rang out from behind the counter where she was arranging a stack of new hardcovers. The older woman's silver hair was bluntly cut in a style that was as fashionable as always. Her glasses were perched on her nose, but of course, they were a vibrant pink color with bedazzled jewels on the ends of the cat-eye shape. She smiled warmly. "I thought you'd forgotten this place existed."

Whitney smiled, her shoulders relaxing immediately. She loved bookstores. "Hey Clemmy. I'm sorry, I haven't forgotten. I've just been so busy."

"Busy, huh? Well, then, if you're here, I bet that you're looking for more than just a good read." She stepped out from around the counter, smoothing her blouse as she approached. "What brings you in today, honey?"

Whitney hesitated, her gaze wandering over to the rows of neatly organized bookshelves. She pulled on the strap of her purse before finally looking at Clemmy. "I was kind of hoping you might have something, I don't know, more practical, like a book about starting a business."

Clemmy raised an eyebrow. "Well, now this is interesting. What kind of business are we talking about?"

Whitney smiled. "A wellness studio, like for yoga, meditation, nutrition workshops. I've been thinking about doing this for years, but lately, it's really starting to feel like a possibility."

"Well, I'll be darned, a wellness studio in Jubilee.

You know, that's exactly what this town could use. Far too many people are eating unhealthy diets. Let me see what we can find."

Whitney followed her to the section near the back of the store, which had shelves filled with books about business, self-help, and entrepreneurship.

Clemmy's eyes scanned over the titles as she muttered to herself, her fingers brushing over the spines. "Let me see, let me see," she said to herself. "Oh, here we go." She pulled a book off the shelf and handed it to Whitney. "This one is about starting a business on a small budget. You know, practical steps, tips, that sort of thing."

Whitney looked at the book, reading the title aloud: *From Dream to Reality: Opening Your Own Business Without Breaking the Bank.* She smiled. "This one actually looks perfect. Thank you, Clemmy."

"Oh, I'm not done yet," Clemmy said with a wink. "Now, this one is about wellness businesses. A little more niche, but I think it might give you some ideas for marketing."

Whitney took the second book and flipped through the pages. "You're a lifesaver. I really didn't think I could find anything like this here."

Clemmy crossed her arms. "Honey, you'd be surprised at what you can find if you know where to look. Now, let me tell you something. Books are only part of the equation. The rest of it comes from here." She tapped a hand over her heart. "You've got to believe in yourself. No book is going to be able to do that for you."

Whitney nodded, clutching the books to her chest. "I know. It's just been tough because my dad thinks this is a ridiculous idea."

Clemmy sighed and leaned against the bookshelf. "Your daddy's a good man. I've known him almost my whole life, but he's as old-fashioned as they come. You know, he's used to having things the way they've always been, and anything new feels like a threat. But that doesn't mean you shouldn't try."

"I just feel like I'm letting him down. He's all I've had since my mom passed, and I know he wants what's best for me, but sometimes it feels like he really wants what's best for him."

Clemmy put a hand on Whitney's arm. "I know he wants what's best for you, sweetie, but sometimes what's best for you doesn't look the same to him. You've got to go out there and live your life for you, not for somebody else."

Whitney had heard the same advice from multiple people now. It was hard to believe that it was okay for her to step out on her own regardless of what her father thought. She felt ridiculous for being in her 30s and caring that much about what he thought, but they had been so close since she was a child that it was hard to imagine him not approving of her. "I don't know how to make him understand."

"You don't have to make him understand. He's the dad. He's the parent. It's his job to figure it out, not yours. You have to do what's right for you, and he'll come around eventually. But don't you put your dreams on hold waiting for his approval."

She nodded. "Thank you. I really needed to hear that today."

"Anytime," Clemmy said. "Now, are you sticking with these two books, or do you want to browse a little more?"

Whitney laughed softly. "I think this is a good start. I don't want to get overwhelmed. I've got plenty to think about already."

Clemmy walked her back to the counter and rang up the books. As she placed them in the bag, she leaned forward. "You've got something special in you, Whitney. Don't you let anyone, not even your daddy, talk you out of it."

"Thanks. It means more than you know."

"Of course, sugar. Now, go out there and start making those dreams happen because one day you'll be old like me, and you'll look back and think about those chances that you wish you'd taken."

Whitney smiled and left the bookstore feeling lighter than she had in days. She walked down the sidewalk with the cool mountain air brushing against her cheeks and looked at the books in her bag. For the first time, her wellness studio really didn't feel like a fantasy. Between Tate helping her with a business plan, Madeline encouraging her, and Clemmy finding her the perfect books, it suddenly felt like a real possibility.

Whitney pushed open the door to the diner, thankful for a little break. It had been another long day at the clinic, but she had agreed to help her father during the dinner rush. Coop always closed the diner down for an hour or two between lunch and dinner to give the kitchen staff time to clean up and prep, but it was unusually quiet today.

She frowned, looking toward the counter where Coop was usually perched with a coffee cup in hand. Today, however, he was sitting at one of the booths instead, his arms crossed tightly over his chest. His jaw was set, and his lips were pressed into a thin line.

Oh, how she knew that look. There were so many times in high school when she had snuck out or done something he found offensive, only to come home and find him sitting just like that in his recliner.

"Hey, Daddy," she called softly, hanging her purse on the hook behind the counter.

He didn't look up, just stared at the table in front of him.

Lately, she had been worried about him. His blood pressure had been high again at his last doctor's appointment, and he kept refusing to take medication.

"Everything okay?" she asked, approaching him cautiously.

"Well, that depends," he said curtly, finally looking up at her. His expression was hard, and it made her stomach twist.

"What's going on? Did something happen?"

Coop let out a humorless laugh, shaking his head. "You tell me, Whitney Faith. Anything you want to share?"

Her heart skipped a beat. "What do you mean?"

"I mean," he said, standing up, "I had some customers in here today talking about you. Said they saw you over at the cafe having lunch with Tate Morgan. Then another one said they saw you and Tate together at Perky's having coffee the other day."

Whitney froze, searching for the right words in her brain but unable to find them.

It had been a mistake to keep this from her father. She was acting like a terrified child. It wasn't as if he was going to hurt her—he had always been kind and loving, even if he was opinionated.

"Well?" Coop demanded. "Is it true?"

She swallowed hard, realizing there was no point in lying. "Yes, it's true. I've met Tate, and we've had coffee and lunch."

"Apparently," Coop said, his face reddening. "Why would you go behind my back like that? You know what that man's doing to my business, to me, and you're over there breaking bread with him?"

"Daddy, it's not like that. Tate isn't trying to hurt you. He's just running his own business like you are. I don't understand why you can't see that. It's not like he came to Jubilee to ruin Coop's Home Cookin'. He didn't even know about this place when he started his business."

"Don't you defend him to me," Coop barked. "I've been running this diner for four decades. I've seen people come and go, but this guy—this guy is taking my customers, my livelihood, and now he's got my own daughter on his side."

"I'm not on his side," she said firmly. "There are

no sides. I'm just trying to figure things out for myself, and Tate's been supportive."

"Supportive?" Coop scoffed. "Supportive of just what, exactly?"

She hesitated. "Of my dreams, Daddy. My wellness studio. He's been helping me come up with a business plan."

The silence that followed her words was deafening. It felt like a boulder was pressing down on her.

Her father stared at her as if she had just slapped him across the face.

"You've been talking to him about that nonsense? Behind my back?"

"It's not nonsense," she said firmly, her hands trembling. "It's something you know I've wanted to do for years, and Tate understands. He believes in me."

"Oh, and I don't?" Coop shot back, his voice cracking. "Is that what you're trying to say?"

"No, I'm not saying that," Whitney said, her eyes stinging with tears that threatened to fall. "But you don't support this. You've made that *so* clear. All you care about is me either staying at the clinic or coming to run the diner—doing what you think is best for me. But what about what I want for my own life?"

"What you want?" Coop's voice rose again. "What

about loyalty, Whitney? What about family? I've been busting my back, keeping this place going all my life just so you'd have something to fall back on. And now you want to throw it all away for some new-age fad?"

Whitney flinched. "It's not a fad. It's my future. I'm sorry if that doesn't fit your idea of what I should be doing, but I won't keep living my life trying to make you happy."

He shook his head, and she couldn't tell if it was anger, hurt, or a mixture of both that crossed his face.

"You have a lot of nerve saying that to me after everything I've done for you."

"I appreciate everything you've done for me, Daddy. I really do. But I'm not going to put my dreams on hold any longer just because you don't believe in them."

They stared at each other for a long moment, tension thick in the air like a Blue Ridge morning fog.

Finally, Whitney broke the silence. "I think I need to leave," she said, her voice barely above a whisper. "I can't keep having this same argument with you."

"Fine," Coop said, turning away. "You go do whatever you want. Clearly, you've already made up your mind."

The words cut deeper than she expected, but she didn't reply.

She walked behind the counter, grabbed her purse, and left the diner, the friendly little bell jingling above her head as it swung shut behind her.

The crisp mountain air hit her in the face, but it did little to cool the fire burning in her chest.

She didn't know how she was going to fix this, but she decided at that moment that it might not be her responsibility to do so.

Whitney balanced a tray of sweet tea pitchers as she helped set up the community potluck. There were long tables filled with covered dishes already, and the air was filled with laughter and chatter. This was one of her favorite Jubilee events, where everyone came together to share food and quality time. She had even convinced her dad to come, even though she knew he was still brooding about Tate's cafe and the fact that she was becoming friends with him.

Her thoughts shifted to Tate. She couldn't stop herself from looking toward the entrance, wondering if he was actually going to show up. She told him earlier in the week about the potluck, and even Brady said he'd invited him, but Tate coming to a town gathering felt like throwing gasoline on an already simmering fire with her father.

Just then, she spotted Tate walking in, balancing two large containers in his hands. He looked around the crowd until his eyes landed on hers, and he smiled. Her stomach did some kind of ridiculous flip that it always did when he was around. She set down her tray and waved him over.

"You made it," she said, setting down the tray.

"I told you I would," he said with a grin. "I figured this was a good time to let folks try what I've been working on."

"So what did you bring?" she asked, looking at the containers.

"Vegan chili and cornbread," he said. "I kept it simple, like you suggested."

"Well, it smells great," Whitney said. She pointed at an open space on one of the tables. He set the containers down.

Across the square, she saw her father by the dessert table, his arms crossed, watching her and Tate. His expression darkened.

"My dad's here."

Tate followed her gaze and nodded toward her father. "Well, I figured he'd be. Don't worry, I'm not going to start any trouble."

She sighed. "I know. It's not you I'm worried about, but I know him, and he won't make this easy."

"Well, then I guess I'm just gonna have to handle it," Tate said, his voice calm as always. Whitney wasn't sure what impressed her more, his confidence or his ability to just stay serene when facing Coop's icy glares.

People began lining up to sample the food. Whitney stayed near Tate's dishes, interested to see how the town would respond. A couple of people approached hesitantly, ladling small portions of chili into their little styrofoam bowls. Whitney watched as they took bites. Their expressions shifted from cautious to pleasantly surprised.

"You know, this is actually pretty good," one of them said. "You'd never know it was vegan."

Tate smiled but remained modest, thanking everyone who tried it. More people came, and his containers were half-empty before he knew it.

Her father, however, did not move from his spot. He seemed determined to ignore Tate's presence altogether. Whitney wanted to intervene to smooth things over somehow, but she just wasn't sure how to bridge that gap. But Tate apparently had no such hesitation.

She watched in shock as he walked straight toward Coop, who was standing by a table full of pecan pies. Whitney ran around the corner so she could hear them.

"Mr. Cooper," Tate said, "I wanted to thank you for coming tonight."

Coop turned, his expression hard. "Well, I wasn't about to miss the potluck, now was I? After all, I've been in Jubilee my entire life."

"Of course," Tate said, unfazed. "I'm glad you're here, and I wanted to say how much I admire what you've built with Coop's Home Cookin'. It's very clear how much this town loves your place."

Whitney held her breath, watching her father's face. His scowl remained firmly in place.

"You know, you've got some nerve," he said. "Coming here and acting like we're buddy-buddy when you've been taking my customers."

"I'm not trying to take anything from you, sir," Tate said. "I think there's room for both of us in Jubilee. People need comfort food, and they also need healthier options. We both serve the same community."

Coop's jaw tightened. "You think you have everything figured out, don't you?"

"Not at all," Tate said. "I just want to be a part of the community, not fight against it. I want you to know I respect what you've done here. I hope you can respect what I'm doing."

Instead of saying anything, Coop turned away and crossed his arms, staring off into the distance. Tate quietly walked away, back to the table.

"Well, you tried," Whitney said softly, meeting him there. "That's more than most people would have done."

He nodded. "It's a start."

CHAPTER 7

Whitney sat at a small corner table in Perky's with her notebook in front of her. She loved this notebook. It had a pink leather cover with embossed gold lettering, and she was using her favorite pen. She considered it to be her lucky pen, although so far, it hadn't brought her any real luck. The coffee shop was busy today with an afternoon crowd, but she had managed to find a quieter spot by the window. She flipped through her notes, looking at pages filled with scribbles and ideas that she had jotted down after reading the books Clemmy had recommended.

She was so nervous at the thought of seeing Tate again. Something about being around him made her nervous every single time. Their last few meetings had been about the business plan, but there was something about him, something that made her feel seen in a way that she hadn't in a long time, or maybe ever.

The door opened, and she looked up to see him walking in. He spotted her immediately and waved. He walked up to the counter, ordered his coffee, and then met her at the table. He always looked so effortlessly put together in his button-down shirts and jeans, and he carried his own leather-bound notebook under one arm.

"Hey," he said, sliding into a seat across from her. "You got the perfect spot in here today."

"Hey," she said, smiling. "I wanted to get a head start, so I got here about half an hour ago, just trying to make sense of everything I've read and all that we've talked about."

He set his notebook on the table and nodded. "Let me see what you've got there."

She hesitated a moment but then pushed her notebook across the table. He flipped through the pages, his eyebrows furrowing as he read.

"You've got a lot of good ideas here. You've really thought this through."

"Thanks," she said. "I just don't know if it's going to be good enough for a successful business."

"It's more than enough," he said firmly. "But we can make it even stronger, I think." He pulled out his own notebook and started jotting down suggestions. "All right, so let's talk location. Have you thought about where you'd want your studio to be?"

"Well, I was thinking somewhere near the square. Maybe not quite on the square, but near it. That way, it's central to everything, so people can walk to it after work or while they're running errands."

"That's a great idea, and you're right. Being close to the square will make it easier for people to find you. What about prices? Have you decided on membership fees or individual class rates? Have you checked into other wellness studios in other areas to see what they're charging?"

"Well, I was thinking of offering both member-ship and individual. You know, membership for people who want to come regularly, but then single-class drop-in options for tourists or people who just want to try it out."

"Very smart," he said, his pen quickly moving across the page. "You're already thinking like a busi-ness owner."

She smiled, feeling pride. "I've been trying to think of everything, but it's hard to know if I'm on the right track."

"Well, you are," he said in his always reassuring tone. "Some things in business you just have to find out while you're doing it. You can't plan for everything, but just know if you hit any roadblocks, we'll figure them out together."

Their eyes met across the table, and Whitney felt a warmth spread through her chest. She quickly looked away.

"So, have you thought about how to market the studio?" he asked, breaking the moment.

"I was thinking about social media, of course, but I'm not really good at that kind of stuff."

"I can help you with that. We can set up an Instagram page, post pictures of the space, maybe even run some promotions to get people excited."

"You make it all sound so easy," she said with a laugh.

"Oh, it's not, but it's worth it."

They spent the next hour talking about the finer details of her plan. Tate offered all kinds of practical and thoughtful advice while she found herself feeling more confident by the minute. As they worked, her thoughts kept drifting back to her father. She hadn't seen him much since their argument at the diner, except for the brief, tense moment at the potluck. She hadn't even worked any shifts lately. His absence weighed on her more than she wanted to admit.

"Hey," Tate said suddenly. "You okay? You seem a little distracted."

She looked up, realizing she'd been staring at her coffee cup. "I'm sorry, I've just been thinking about my dad. Things have been rough between us lately."

"I figured. He's a tough guy, but it's very clear that he loves you."

"I know. I just don't think he understands how much this whole thing means to me. I'm worried about him. His health is not great, and all this stress is not helping."

Tate reached across the table and placed a hand over hers. It sent a jolt of warmth through her.

"You're doing the right thing, Whitney. I know it's hard, but sometimes we have to make choices for ourselves, even if it's not what other people want."

"Thank you."

"Anytime," he said, giving her hand a gentle squeeze before pulling back. She felt an immediate void.

"Now, let's finish this plan. You've got a wellness studio to open."

They went back to work, but the weight on Whitney's chest felt a little bit lighter. At least Tate believed in her, and for now, that had to be enough.

As they wrapped up their meeting and she told him goodbye, she felt a sense of hope. Her relationship with her father was strained, for sure, but she was determined to prove to him and herself that she could make this dream a reality.

Whitney pulled on the strap of her backpack as she followed Madeline up the steep and winding trail. The sound of the leaves crunched beneath their feet. The air outside was crisp and cool, and it was the kind of morning that promised sunshine later but still held on to the chill of the Blue Ridge Mountains. In front of them, Geneva led the way, her pace brisk despite her age. She expertly navigated the uneven terrain like she did it every day —and she probably did.

"I do not know how in the world you convinced me to do this," Whitney said, laughing as she looked at Madeline.

"Listen, you've been stuck in that clinic or at the diner for weeks," Madeline said, pulling a stray branch out of the way. "A little fresh air won't kill you."

Geneva laughed, glancing over her shoulder. "Says the famous romance novelist that I practically had to drag out here every single time for those first few months."

Madeline chuckled. "I was a different woman back then."

"Whitney, if you can't keep up, honey, just say so," Geneva said, glancing over her shoulder again.

Whitney rolled her eyes. "Are you trying to make me look bad, Geneva? But seriously, don't you ever get tired?"

"Not when I'm out here," Geneva said, stopping and holding her hands up toward the trees. "There's nothing like being in the mountains to remind you of what life is all about. You know, your daddy used to say the same thing when we were kids, though I'm sure he's forgotten by now. I don't ever see him wandering around out in the woods. He seems to stay in that diner twenty-four hours a day."

Whitney nodded. "Yes, he does, and it's affecting his health."

Geneva looked at her with concern. "His health? What's going on?"

"Oh, he's been having trouble with his blood pressure for months. I keep telling him to take the medicine the doctor is prescribing, but he won't do it. Says he doesn't want to be stuck on a bunch of pills. And now he's so stressed out about the vegan cafe that his face is always red, and I know if I checked his blood pressure, it would probably be off the charts."

"Sometimes it's hard to deal with loved ones. We can't make them do what we want them to do—and often what they need to do. It's very frustrating. I don't want anything bad to happen to him."

Geneva waved her hand. "Now, I know this is a serious topic, but we won't let it derail us from our hike. This is meant to make you feel more clear-headed and calm. Talking about problems that you can't control isn't going to do that."

They started walking again.

"But you've known my dad a long time, right?" Whitney asked.

Geneva chuckled. "Longer than you've been alive," she said. "Oh, he was a wild one back in those days. I always thought he'd leave Jubilee and go out and see the world, but when your mama came along, he decided there was no reason to go anywhere else."

Whitney felt a pang in her chest. Her mother's passing had been such a turning point for her father, and she had always wondered how different it might have been if her mother had survived her cancer.

"Did you ever think about leaving here?" Whitney asked.

Geneva stopped at a small clearing, motioning for them to take a break. She pulled a water bottle from her pack and took a sip. "I did—plenty of times, actually. I even tried it once. Spent a summer in Nashville when I was about your age, working at a bookstore. I dreamed of a big city life. But you know what? I just missed these mountains too much, so I came back and never regretted it."

Whitney sat down on a fallen log. "I guess I've always felt like I just needed to stay for my dad."

Madeline sat beside her, brushing the dirt off her hands. "You know, there's nothing wrong with loving your family, Whitney. But loving your family doesn't mean putting your dreams on hold forever. They had their chance at their own dreams, and now it's your turn."

Geneva nodded. "Your daddy's one of the most stubborn men I've ever met, I'll give you that. But I've also known Coop long enough to know that in his heart, he wants what's best for you, even if he doesn't know how to show you."

Whitney pulled out her own water bottle and took a long sip. "He thinks my wellness studio is some ridiculous idea. He wants me to either stay at the clinic or work at the diner because they're steady jobs. He thinks I'd be foolish to give them up."

"Steady jobs are fine if that's what you want," Geneva said. "But honey, if your heart's not in it, you'll regret it every day. You'll be sad when you wake up every morning. Coop's just scared. He has spent his whole life trying to make sure you were taken care of, and the idea of you stepping out on your own terrifies him."

"You know, when I first started writing, I had a lot of people tell me it was a waste of time," Madeline said. "Even my husband at the time thought it was silly. But I just kept going because I knew it was what I was meant to be doing. And if I'd listened to everyone else, I wouldn't have written a single book."

"But what if I fail?" Whitney asked, looking at each of them. "What if I sink everything I have into this, and it doesn't work?"

"Then you get back up, and you try again. That's what life's about, Whitney," Geneva said. "You don't get anywhere by sitting still and playing it safe. Your daddy knows that even if he doesn't want to admit it."

"I just don't want to disappoint him. Or maybe it's that I don't want to disappoint myself."

"You're not disappointing anyone," Madeline said. "Taking chances is one of the best parts of life."

They sat in silence for a moment, the wind rustling through the leaves. Then Geneva finally stood. "All right, come on, ladies. Enough of this sitting around. Let's get moving. There's a view up ahead that will remind you why you love this place."

Whitney smiled as she followed the older women in front of her. It was almost a beautiful metaphor. Women who had blazed a trail ahead of her were counting on her now to blaze her own.

Whitney pushed open the door of Jubilee Vegan Cafe and walked inside, holding onto her notebook. She was getting so comfortable here—maybe a little too comfortable. The late afternoon rush had cleared, and the space felt warm and inviting, with soft music playing in the background. Tate was behind the counter, as usual, wiping down the surfaces. He looked up, saw her, and smiled, making her heart skip a beat.

"Hey, Whit," he said, laying the rag aside. "Come on in. I've got the whole place to myself for a couple of hours."

"Great, thanks," she said, her voice a little breathless from hurrying over after her shift at the clinic. She slid into one of the booths, putting her bag and notebook on the table. "You know, I've been working on some ideas. I wanted to run them past you."

He sat down with her a moment later, carrying

two steaming mugs of coffee. "Thought you could use it after a long day."

"You read my mind," she said, wrapping her hands around it and letting the warmth seep into her fingers. "Thank you."

"No problem. So, let's hear what you've got."

She opened her notebook and flipped through the pages filled with scribbled ideas and diagrams. "All right, so I've been thinking about how to make the studio feel more accessible to everyone. You know, not just for people who are already fit and healthy, but for people who might be skeptical, like people of my dad's generation or—"

"People like Coop," he interrupted with a teasing grin.

"Exactly," she said. "I was thinking about offering some beginner-level classes and workshops. You know, maybe a community discount for local people. I just want it to feel like a place for everyone."

He nodded, leaning back in his seat. "That's really smart, and I think it could work, but—" he trailed off, tapping his finger on the table.

"But what?"

He leaned forward, resting on his elbows. "What if you didn't just talk about it—the ideas, I mean? What if you actually tried them out?"

She blinked at him, her pen hanging above the page. "Try it out? How?"

"Here," he said, pointing around the cafe. "Let's host a wellness night. You can use my place as your test run."

Her mouth dropped open. "Seriously? You'd let me do that?"

"Of course, I would," he said with a shrug. "This is the perfect place to do it. We can move the tables over to that side and set up yoga mats or whatever you need. You could do some mindfulness sessions, a nutrition workshop—basically anything you've got in mind. It'll be a great test run. I'll even make some snacks. Something healthy but delicious to show people that that's possible."

She stared at him. "I don't know, Tate. What if nobody shows up? Or what if they think the whole thing is stupid like my dad does?"

"Well, then they're missing out," he said. "But I don't think that's going to happen. I think people are going to show up because you're passionate about this. They're going to feel that. You just need to take this leap."

She bit her lip, her mind racing with the possibilities. The whole idea scared her to death, but she was so excited that it overshadowed the fear. "Okay," she said. "Let's do it. I'll need some time to plan, but this could be just the push I need."

Tate smiled. "That's what I like to hear. You're going to crush this, Whitney. I know it."

She smiled back. "Thank you, Tate, for being the only one who believes in me, it seems."

"Always," he said softly.

A moment hung between them, charged with some kind of electricity she'd never felt before. Whitney cleared her throat and looked back down at her notes. "Okay, then, so let's talk logistics."

For the next hour, they worked together, eating snacks and hammering out details for the event. Tate offered all kinds of marketing ideas, suggesting they put up flyers at Perky's and the library, while Whitney made notes about which activities she wanted to include. At one point, their hands brushed against each other as they both reached for the pen, and she felt a jolt that left her breathless.

"Sorry," he said, his eyes locking on hers.

"It's fine," she said quickly, her cheeks burning. She focused again on her notebook.

When they wrapped up, Whitney felt a mixture of excitement and nerves. She gathered her things, and Tate walked her to the door.

"You're going to do great," he said, his voice low

and steady. "I can't wait to see what you come up with."

"Thank you," she said, looking up at him. For a minute, she thought he was going to lean in closer, but then the door jingled as she pushed it open, breaking the moment. She stepped out into the cool evening air, her heart still racing, clutching her notebook to her chest. Her dream was starting to feel more and more like a reality.

CHAPTER 8

Coop stood behind the counter of his beloved diner, refilling a pot of coffee as the hum of distant customer chatter filled the space. The lunch rush had just begun, and Wanda was bustling back and forth between the tables, trying to balance plates of fried chicken and collard greens with her usual efficiency. His eyes scanned the room, taking in the familiar faces of locals who had been eating there for years, some of them for decades.

He focused on wiping down the counter when a snippet of conversation from a nearby table suddenly caught his attention.

"What's a wellness night? And it's over at the vegan place?" a woman said, her voice full of curiosity.

"Yeah," the other customer replied. "I saw a flyer at Perky's this morning. It says Whitney is hosting it with all kinds of stuff like yoga, nutrition tips, and healthy snacks. Can you believe that? That Coop's daughter is teaming up with Tate Morgan? That has to sting."

Coop froze, his hand gripping the rag tightly. His jaw clenched as he turned his ear toward the conversation, trying not to make it obvious that he was eavesdropping.

"Honestly," the woman said, trying to whisper, "it sounds kind of interesting. I'm probably gonna stop by and see what it's all about. I need to lose a little weight, and it's nice to see someone in town doing something new and fresh."

Coop slammed the coffee pot down onto the warmer, causing a loud clatter. The two women stopped talking and looked over at him for a moment before returning to their conversation. His mind was racing.

Wellness night at Tate's cafe, and Whitney was the one hosting it? She hadn't said a word about it to him, not even after they had their blow-up. His own daughter, his flesh and blood, was not only working with the man who was taking his customers away but was doing it secretly. The betrayal felt like a punch in the gut.

Wanda walked over to the counter, carrying a tray of empty plates. Her brow furrowed when she saw the storm brewing on Coop's face.

"What in the world has you all riled up?" she asked, setting the tray on the counter.

"Did you know about this wellness night thing that Whitney's doing with that guy across the street?"

Wanda looked surprised. "Wellness night? No, I can't say that I did. What's the problem?"

Coop pointed toward the table where the customers were still talking. "Apparently, according to these people who talk a little too loudly, my daughter is teaming up with that Tate Morgan, putting on some kind of event at his cafe. Yoga and salads and who knows what else. She didn't even tell me anything about it."

Wanda's expression softened. "Coop, don't go jumping to conclusions. She probably just didn't want to upset you, especially not with everything that's been going on between you two. It's not like you take this kind of news very well."

"You think she was worried about upsetting me?" Coop's voice rose, drawing more glances from nearby tables. He lowered it again. "She knows exactly how I feel about that place over there and that man, and now she's gonna work with him behind my back?"

Wanda sighed, leaning against the counter. "Coop, you and Whitney haven't been on the best of terms lately. You two barely even talk anymore. It's very sad—I've known her since she was born. Maybe she just didn't feel like she could talk to you about it. Now, don't get mad when I say this, but you've kind of gotten a little overwrought about that new place."

"That's because she's siding with him," Coop said bitterly. "Ever since he showed up in this town, it's been nothing but trouble. Now he's got my daughter on his side, helping him to run me out of business. What did I ever do to make her hate me so much?"

"Oh, you stop it," Wanda said sharply. "Tate is not running you out of business, Coop. You acting like this—especially in front of customers—and ruining your relationship with your daughter is what's going to run you out of business. He's trying to make a living, same as you, and Whitney isn't siding with anyone. She wants to chase her own dreams, even if you don't support them. Maybe you ought to stop and think about just how hard that must be for her, knowing that her father, who she loves dearly, doesn't even support her."

Coop opened his mouth to argue, but Wanda held up her hand to stop him. "And don't you roll your eyes at me," she said firmly. "You're so caught up in your own pride that you don't even see the bigger picture. Whitney adores you. She always has. You're her only family, but she's not a little girl anymore. That's a grown woman with dreams of her own, and instead of tearing her down, maybe you ought to be building her up."

He scowled, looking down at the counter. "You don't understand, Wanda. This diner, this is all I've got. It's all I've ever known, and now she's walking away from it—and me."

"She's not walking away from you. She's walking toward something that makes her happy. That doesn't mean she loves you any less. Although, if you don't stop acting like a horse's butt, you're going to run her away to where she never comes back."

He sighed heavily, rubbing his hand over his face. Deep down—very deep down—he knew Wanda was right, but that didn't make it any less painful. He'd always thought that Whitney would stay close, that she'd want to carry on the legacy he'd built. The idea of her choosing a totally different path, especially one that felt like it aligned her with Tate, felt like a personal betrayal.

"So then, what am I supposed to do, Wanda? Just let it all happen?"

"You're supposed to support her, Coop, even if

it's hard, even if it hurts—because that's what being a parent is about."

He nodded slowly, but the frustration still lingered. Wanda patted his arm and then picked up her tray to take it to the back.

"Now, why don't you just take a minute and think about what you're gonna say to Whitney, because if you go storming up to her with that temper of yours, you're only gonna make things worse."

He watched her walk away and push open the swinging doors to the kitchen, her words echoing in his mind. He didn't know how in the world he would fix things with his daughter, but one thing was for sure: he couldn't ignore this situation any longer.

W hitney looked at herself in the bathroom mirror at the clinic, adjusting her hair a bit before shaking her head. This was not a date. It was just a dinner—a casual dinner with Tate. It was nothing more. She'd spent the afternoon with him at the cafe, hammering out all the details for wellness night, but he had suggested that maybe they go grab a bite to eat. Her stomach fluttered at the thought, but she was going to push those feelings aside. He didn't feel that way about her. He was just being nice. This wasn't a date, she reminded herself yet again.

When she arrived at the Buzzed Bear, a cozy little tavern on the edge of town, Tate was already waiting near the entrance. He looked relaxed in his navy button-down shirt and jeans, and he had an easy smile on his face when he saw her.

"Hey," he said, holding the door open. "Glad you made it."

"Of course," she said, walking past him, feeling the faintest tingle of awareness as his arm hovered near hers. She could smell his cologne. He had put it on since they'd met in the afternoon. Did that mean anything?

"I was starving after all that planning," she said, laughing.

The Buzzed Bear was bustling as it usually was, laughter and the low hum of conversation filling the space. There were strings of twinkle lights hanging across the ceiling between the wooden beams. There was such a rustic charm about this place, and she loved going there when she had a chance. After all, they had the best chicken fingers in town—although

she would never tell that to her father. They had
pool tables and a big bar with a stuffed bear behind
all the bottles of various alcohol.

They found a small booth near the back, away
from the crowd.

"So, do you come here often?" Whitney asked as
she looked at the menu.

"I've been a few times since moving here. They
have a wonderful Cobb salad, and there's a good vibe
here. Their black bean burger is actually pretty
amazing, too."

"Let me guess, you don't eat any fries?"

"Hey, I'm not that strict," he said with a laugh. "I
have some fries now and then. Life's all about
balance. But, you know, I make fries without any oil
in my air fryer, and they're just as good if you season
them well."

"Interesting," she said, smiling and looking down
at her menu.

They placed their order, Tate sticking with his
black bean burger and Whitney opting for a chicken
club sandwich, and then fell into an easy
conversation.

"So," Tate said, resting his elbows on the table,
"we've been talking about wellness night and the
plans for that nonstop, but let's take a break. I want

to know more about you. What was it like growing up here in Jubilee?"

She smiled, leaning back as the memories of her childhood flooded forward in her mind. "It was great, actually, really great. My dad—he's always been a larger-than-life character, you know. Everyone in town knows him, and he's always been very proud of the diner. He used to bring me there when I was little and teach me how to fold napkins and refill salt shakers."

"Sounds like you two have always been close," Tate said.

"Well, we were," Whitney said softly. "I guess we still are, even if things have been a little strained lately. He's a good man, though. He worked so hard to build the diner from the ground up, and he took care of me after my mom passed away. He's got the best sense of humor, always cracking jokes, even when things are tough."

He nodded. "It's clear how much you care about him. I can tell he's important to you."

"He is, but I'm worried about him. His blood pressure has been up for years, and he won't take it seriously—he refuses to take medication. I'm scared that one day, it's going to catch up with him."

Tate reached across the table, his hand brushing hers for a moment before he pulled back. "That's tough, Whitney. I can see why you'd be worried. But, you know, maybe with all the stuff you're working on, like the wellness night, he'll come around. He'll see you're not just doing this for yourself but for people just like him."

She smiled. "Thank you. I hope so, but I think that's probably a pipe dream."

Their food arrived, and they ate for a while in comfortable silence before Tate spoke again.

"I think I told you this, but," he said, putting his burger back down on the plate, "this whole healthy living thing started with my grandma. She had diabetes, and it really affected her quality of life. Watching her struggle was what got me interested in nutrition and wellness. I wanted to do something to help people avoid what she went through because diabetes is very much treatable with diet and exercise."

"That's amazing. I think she'd be proud of what you're doing."

"Thanks. Sometimes I wonder if it's enough, but hearing you say that helps."

For a moment, they just stared at each other, the noise of the tavern fading into the background.

"So," she said, breaking the silence, "do you always get this deep on a not-date?"

He leaned forward. "Oh, this is a not-date, huh? Is that what it is?"

She shrugged. "Well, it's not a date. I mean, we're just two people grabbing dinner after work, right?"

"Right," he said, a teasing smile on his lips. "But if it were a date, would you be okay with that?"

Her breath hitched in her throat, and she struggled to find the right response. Before she could say anything, the waitress approached the table with the check and asked if they wanted dessert. They both said no, and Tate took care of the bill, waving off her protests before they stepped out into the evening air.

"Thanks for dinner," Whitney said as they walked toward her car.

"Anytime. I meant what I said earlier. You're doing something really special, Whitney. Don't let anyone make you think otherwise."

"You're not so bad yourself, Tate Morgan," she said as they stopped at her car.

He smiled, and for a moment, she thought he might step closer. The air between them felt charged, and her heart started to pound. Instead, he stepped back and put his hands in his pockets.

"Well, good night, Whitney."

"Good night," she said softly before she climbed into her car and then watched him walk toward his.

It wasn't a date. It couldn't have been a date. Well, maybe—just maybe—it could have been.

Whitney wiped down a booth at the diner between the breakfast and lunch rush. She hadn't been working much at the diner lately, but when Wanda called to say she had a server out sick and really needed the help—and promised that Coop was not around—Whitney agreed to go.

A couple of regulars were sipping their coffee, and their conversation drifted just loud enough for her to catch snippets.

"So, did you see the review online?" a gray-haired man named Frank said with a chuckle. "Coop's really got one over on that vegan guy."

Whitney's hand froze mid-swipe, her heart sinking. She forced herself to continue cleaning so that she could hear more, but she had to strain her ear to do so.

"Oh yeah," his friend replied. "I heard old Coop's been talking to folks, asking them to post some stuff about that vegetable café—you know, show some loyalty to this place."

Whitney felt her stomach twist into a knot. This couldn't be true, could it? Her father had been vocal about his dislike for Tate's café, but asking people to leave bad reviews? Well, that just wasn't like him. She thought it wasn't, at least.

She finished wiping the table and walked back behind the counter, her mind racing. Wanda was at the coffee station refilling pots. Whitney hesitated for a moment before stepping closer.

"Hey, Wanda," she said quietly. "Can I ask you something?"

"Sure, honey, what's up?" Wanda said, turning around and putting her hands on her hips.

"Have you heard anything about my dad asking people to leave bad reviews about Tate's café?"

Wanda paused, her lips pressing together in a thin line.

"Now Whitney, I don't want to get in the middle of anything, but I did hear him mention something about that the other day. He was venting about how people are going over there, and I guess he figured if some people saw negative stuff online, it might just slow things down a bit."

Whitney's shoulders sagged. "I can't believe this. My dad has always been so proud of owning a legit business. Honesty was a huge thing that he taught me. Why would he do something like this?"

Wanda gave her a sympathetic look. "Honey, your daddy is scared. He's never had any real competition before, and I think he's feeling desperate. Sure doesn't make it right, though. I lit into him the other day about this very thing."

Whitney didn't want to believe it, but she couldn't ignore what she'd heard. She looked at the clock. Her shift at the clinic started in an hour. She was working in the evening, but she couldn't focus on work with this weighing on her. She wasn't going to confront her father right away, but she decided she needed to tell Tate. He deserved to know.

"Listen, Wanda, I know you need help, but I've got to go."

Wanda nodded knowingly. "I understand. And for what it's worth, I think he's a nice guy, that Tate. He brought some vegan muffins by here one day, and they were delicious. I was very surprised."

Whitney smiled and nodded. "He's a wonderful guy, and he's been a great help to me. I just wish my dad could see that."

She took off her apron, picked up her purse, and ran out the front door, heading straight across the street. She found Tate standing behind the counter, as usual, chatting with a customer.

"Hey, Whitney, what brings you by?"

"Can we talk?" she asked, her voice low. "I mean, privately."

His brow furrowed, but he nodded, leading her

to a small table in the corner. He pulled out a chair for her before sitting across from her.

"What's up?" he asked, obviously concerned.

She fidgeted with the strap of her purse, hesitating. "I don't even know how to say this because it's honestly very embarrassing, but I overheard something today, and I think you need to know about it."

He leaned forward. "Okay."

She took a deep breath. "So, I heard some customers over at the diner talking about how my dad has asked people to leave bad reviews for your café online. Wanda kind of confirmed it."

Tate's expression didn't change immediately, but then she saw a flicker of disappointment in his eyes. He leaned back in his chair and let out a long breath.

"I figured something was going on when I saw a couple of those reviews. They seemed off, like they weren't from real people who had been here. I guess I just didn't think your dad would go that far."

"I'm so sorry, Tate," she said, her voice barely above a whisper. "This isn't the dad I've always known. I didn't know he was doing this, and I certainly don't agree with it. I just thought you should know."

Tate nodded. "It's not your fault, Whitney. I know you're in a tough spot, stuck between him and me, and I appreciate you coming here to tell me."

"I don't know what to do," she admitted. "Part of me wants to go confront him right now, but I don't think he's going to listen. He's so stubborn, and I'm afraid it's just going to make this whole thing worse. But I can't let him continue to have people leave these reviews."

He reached across the table and rested his hand on top of hers. "You don't have to do anything right now. This is something I'll handle. Your dad's scared, I get that. I just hope he realizes we're not enemies. We're just two people trying to make a living."

Whitney felt so guilty. "He's not a bad person, Tate. I know you probably don't believe that right now, but he's just been under so much stress lately, and I think he's worried about losing everything he's worked for."

"I know, and I'm not here to take anything away from him, including you. I just wish he'd see that."

That comment made her stomach feel fluttery, but she had to ignore it right now. There was a heavy weight sitting on top of both of them.

Finally, Tate smiled slightly. "Thank you for telling me. That decision couldn't have been easy for you."

"It wasn't," Whitney admitted. "But you deserve to know. And if there's anything I can do to help, please let me know."

"You've already helped," he said, his hand lingering a moment longer before pulling it away.

Whitney left the café and walked toward her car with a mix of relief and anxiety. She knew she had done the right thing by telling him, but this rift between her and her father felt wider than the Grand Canyon right now, and she didn't know how they would ever build a bridge back to each other.

CHAPTER 9

The little bell above the door jingled as Madeline, Whitney, and Clemmy stepped inside of Whisk Me Away, the cozy little bakery nestled in the heart of the Square of Jubilee. There was a warm scent of vanilla and freshly baked pastries that wrapped around them like a hug as they walked inside. The glass display case was packed with everything from towering layered cakes to delicate chocolate eclairs. Frannie herself was running around behind the counter with her apron dusted with flour. She had her signature messy bun threatening to unravel from the top of her head. She looked up and waved.

"Well, look if it isn't my favorite trio," Frannie said. "What can I get y'all today?"

Clemmy walked up first, looking at the desserts

with the scrutiny of a jeweler inspecting diamonds. "Frannie, you have outdone yourself here. I think I'll take a slice of that lemon lavender cake and a cup of your very strongest coffee."

"Coming right up," Frannie said, writing down the order. "What about you, Madeline?"

"I think I'll have the chocolate espresso torte with the raspberry topping and just some green tea, please."

"And you, hun? Don't tell me you're skipping out on dessert."

Whitney laughed softly and shook her head. "Oh, I wouldn't dare. I'll have a slice of that strawberry shortcake and a caramel latte."

The three women went and took a seat by the window. Clemmy leaned back in her chair, tapping her fingers on the table. "Now, this is what I call a proper ladies' outing. Cake, coffee, and no men around to interrupt us."

Madeline laughed. "Speak for yourself. I think Brady would be perfectly happy to interrupt us right now if it meant that he could get a bite of that torte."

"True," Clemmy said with a smile. "But let's focus on the important things. Like Whitney here and her little cafe buddy."

Whitney blinked, caught in mid-sip of her latte. "Excuse me?"

"You heard me," Clemmy said playfully. "Word is, you've been spending a lot of time with that very healthy Tate fella, planning some fancy wellness night. Is that true?"

Madeline raised an eyebrow. "Well, well, Whitney, is there something you want to share with the class?"

Whitney groaned. "It's not like that. You've probably seen the flyer, so it's not like I was trying to keep a secret. Tate's just been helping me with my business plan, that's all. He's just a good friend."

Clemmy smirked, cutting into her piece of lavender cake. "Honey, I've been around this earth long enough to know when something's more than just a friend. The way you're blushing right now tells me everything I need to know."

Whitney felt her cheeks burn and looked at Madeline for support, but Madeline just shrugged. "Clemmy's not wrong. Every time you talk about him, your face lights up like a Christmas tree."

"That's just not true," Whitney protested.

"Sure, it's not," Clemmy said. "Let me ask you this. When was the last time you spent this much time with a man and actually enjoyed it?"

Whitney hesitated. The truth was, she couldn't remember. Between working at the clinic, helping her dad, and her own self-doubt, she hadn't made very much room for relationships in her life. But with Tate, things felt very different.

"It doesn't matter. My focus is on the wellness studio. That is all I have time for right now."

"Whitney, nobody's saying you have to dive into anything," Madeline said, leaning forward. "But it's okay to let yourself feel something, to open yourself up to the possibility of more. You deserve that."

Clemmy nodded. "Madeline's right, sweetie. You've got so much on your plate, but that doesn't mean there's no room for dessert if you catch my drift."

Whitney rolled her eyes but couldn't help but laugh. "You two are relentless, you know that?"

"Absolutely," Clemmy said. "It's why we're here. The elder statesmen, or stateswomen, I guess, of the city. Here to help you make good life choices and offer you our wisdom."

"Everything taste good, ladies?" Frannie asked as she walked to the table.

"Perfect," Madeline said. "Frannie, you're a genius."

"As usual," Clemmy added, letting out an exaggerated sigh of delight.

As Frannie walked back behind the counter, Clemmy looked at Whitney. "You know, I'm gonna tell you something. I don't often talk about my personal life. And that's probably because there really isn't much of one. It's been many years since I even went on a date. I gave up on the idea of love a long time ago and dove headfirst into running the bookstore. But let me tell you something. The older I get, the lonelier I get. I haven't seen my son in a long time. You know, he's in the military, and he has his own family to focus on. And it's very lonely for somebody who goes home to an empty house every night. You don't want to be that person, Whitney. You don't want to do everything your father expects of you. You need to do the things that make you happy, that fill you up. And if somebody comes along that deserves your love, and you have the same feelings for them, you don't need to let fear stop you."

Madeline reached over and put her hand on Clemmy's. "Clemmy, that was beautiful. And I didn't know you were so lonely. What can we do to help?"

Clemmy waved her hand away. "Oh, honey, I'm used to it. It's been this way for so long. I don't know any other way anymore."

"Well, that makes me sad," Madeline said. "I want you to have what I have with Brady. I never expected a second chance at love. But look at us now."

"What you and Brady have is very special, but it's also like a unicorn. I sure don't expect to walk outside and find one of those walking through the town square now, do I?"

"It makes me sad, too," Whitney said, reaching over for Clemmy's hand.

"Ladies, this is not about me," Clemmy said. "Good Lord, I wish I'd never said anything," she said, taking a sip of her drink. "Let's not talk anymore about it," she said, brushing it away.

"Well, fine, we'll stop talking," Madeline said. "But Whitney, I want you to know you have two of the biggest cheerleaders in Jubilee sitting right here. So whatever happens, with Wellness Night or anything else, we've got your back."

The little bell above the door jingled as Whitney walked into the diner. The lunch rush had just ended, and the room had settled into a deceptive calm. Her father leaned against the counter, his arms crossed and his jaw set tighter than a drum.

Whitney adjusted the strap of her bag, cautious as she approached. She placed it on a hook near the counter and gave him a small, hesitant smile.

"Hey, Daddy," she said softly.

"Don't you 'Hey, Daddy' me," Coop snapped, his

voice sharper than she'd heard it in a while. "We need to talk."

Whitney froze, her eyes narrowing slightly. "What's up?"

"You want to tell me about this wellness night of yours?" Coop pushed off the counter, stepping closer. His face was flushed, and she figured it wasn't just from the heat of the kitchen.

"How did you find out about it?"

"Oh, I've got ears, Whitney," he said. "I heard it from customers. They're all buzzing about how my daughter is putting on some big event over at that man's café."

Whitney sighed, her shoulders slumping. "I wasn't trying to keep it a secret. There have been flyers at Perky's and at the library. If you didn't know, it's because you never leave this place long enough to know about anything else happening around town."

"Don't you put this on me!" Coop shot back, his voice rising. "You knew exactly how I'd feel about it, and you didn't have the guts to just come tell me yourself."

Her temper flared. "Why would I, Dad? So you can explode like this? So you could accuse me of siding with the enemy again? I'm tired of having this same fight over and over. You're being ridiculous!"

"I don't even know who you are anymore!" he shouted, throwing his arms up in frustration.

"Well, maybe if you stopped siding with him, we wouldn't have to fight," Coop said, slamming his hand on the counter. "Do you have any idea how this looks? That my own daughter is teaming up with a guy who's trying to run me out of business?"

Whitney's mouth dropped open in disbelief. "Tate is not trying to run you out of business, Dad! He's trying to make a living, just like you are. You're the one who's turned this into some kind of war. You're the only person fighting!"

Coop's face darkened. "Don't you tell me what this is, Whitney. You're too busy playing business partners with him to see what's really going on."

"And what is that, Daddy?" she shot back, stepping closer. "That maybe, just maybe, the world doesn't revolve around Coop's Home Cookin'? That there's room for something new in this town without it being a personal attack on you? That's pretty self-centered!"

He recoiled as though she'd slapped him. "You think I don't know what this town needs? I've been feeding these people since before you were born. I know what they want, and it sure as heck ain't yoga classes and kale chips."

"And this is exactly why I didn't tell you about

Wellness Night!" Whitney snapped. "You're so stubborn, you can't even hear me out. You just shut me down before I get the chance to explain anything."

"Explain what?" he demanded, his voice booming. "How you're working with him behind my back? How you're putting his business ahead of ours?"

Coop's voice had gotten so loud that Wanda peeked her head out of the kitchen, concern etched across her face.

Whitney's eyes stung with angry tears, but she refused to let them fall. "You want to talk about betrayal, Daddy? Fine. Then let's talk about all those fake reviews you've been having people leave for his café. You think I don't know about that?"

Coop froze, his mouth opening and closing like he was searching for words.

"You're not the man I grew up admiring," she said, her voice breaking. "The man who taught me to work hard and be honest. What happened to you, Daddy? When did you let your pride turn you into someone I don't even recognize anymore?"

"That's enough," he said, holding up his hand to stop her. "You don't get to stand there and judge me —not when you're the one tearing this family apart."

Whitney stepped back, shocked. "Tearing this family apart? You're the one doing that! You're so blinded by your hatred for Tate that you can't even see what it's doing to me and you!"

"I'm trying to protect what's mine," Coop bellowed. "This diner is all I have left, Whitney. You think I want to wake up one day and see it boarded up because some fancy café stole all my customers?"

"Nobody's trying to steal your customers!" she shouted back. "If you spent half as much energy trying to do better things for your own business as you do hating a man who's done nothing to you, maybe you wouldn't be so worried!"

His face hardened. "I see how it is. You think I'm the problem. You think I'm just some old man with nothing left to give, standing in your way."

"You know that's not what I mean!" she said, her voice trembling. "I love you. I just… I need you to see that this isn't about taking sides. This is about your daughter chasing her dreams—finally. But you're too caught up in your own pride to even support me."

Coop shook his head, looking away. "You've made your choice, Whitney. Don't expect me to stand here and cheer you on when it means tearing down everything I've built all these years."

There was a finality in his tone that scared her.

Swallowing hard, Whitney grabbed her bag from the hook. "I can't do this with you right now," she said, her voice quiet but firm. "I've spent my whole life trying to make you proud, but right now, it's time I start trying to make myself proud."

She turned and walked out the door, her chest tight with emotion. As she stepped onto the street, she wondered when—or if—she would even talk to her father again.

W hitney walked into her small apartment, the faint creak of the hinges breaking the silence of the evening. She loved having an apartment on the square. She was on the second floor of a building just above one of the local shops that sold souvenirs to Jubilee visitors. She flipped on the light switch, flooding the room with warm, golden light. She dropped her bag in the entryway, sighed, and took off her coat before hanging it on a hook by the door.

The tension in her shoulders felt like it was never going to let loose. Maybe she should take her own advice and do some yoga stretches before bed.

She walked into the kitchen and filled a kettle with water, placing it on the stove. She was going to make some nice chamomile tea, put on her comfiest pajamas, and veg out in front of the TV for the rest of the evening. At least, that was her plan. But the argument with her father kept replaying in her mind like a broken record, every word cutting deeper and deeper.

The kettle finally whistled, and she poured the hot water over a teabag in her favorite ceramic mug. It had a picture of a cute little raccoon on it, which was her favorite animal. She carried it to the living room and sank into the corner of the overly worn, overstuffed couch. The tea's steam crawled in the air, but she didn't take a sip right away. Instead, she stared at the coffee table in front of her, its surface cluttered with notes and books for Wellness Night.

"Wellness," she said to herself with a hollow laugh. "I can't even handle my own life right now. How in the world am I supposed to teach other people how to have wellness?"

That thought hung in the air, heavy and unyielding. She taught other people about mindfulness, balance, and self-care, and yet here she was with a pounding heart and a mind racing with guilt. Her father's words had stung more than anything she'd ever heard in her life, but what hurt her the most was the distance between them.

She reached for her favorite journal. It was leather-bound and had some scratches on it. The pages inside were filled with her scribbled thoughts, hopes, and fears. She opened it and found a blank page, grabbed her favorite pen, and started to let the words flow.

I miss Mom.

The words were simple, but they evoked so much emotion. Her hand stilled for a moment as emotion bubbled up inside her. Writing them down made them feel more real. She blinked back tears and started writing again.

She would have known what to say to him. She always did. Whenever Daddy and I fought, she was the one who brought us back together. She understood him in a way that I don't think anyone else ever will. I try, but it's like we're speaking two totally different languages. He's so angry now. I don't know how to reach him. I don't know who he is anymore.

She paused, tapping the pen against her lip. Her apartment was so quiet, almost oppressively so. Sometimes, she thought she should get a puppy or maybe even a cat. A puppy would be hard because she lived on the second floor, and she'd have to take it out over and over. Plus, she was rarely home these days. Maybe a cat was better, except she did have an allergy to them, and she would hate to spend most of her time sneezing.

The quiet was hard. She longed for those days when her mother's laughter filled the rooms when the three of them were a family, a team, each other's biggest supporters.

She continued to write.

I miss Daddy, too.

The words surprised her, but they were true. She missed the version of her father who laughed with her, who took her fishing on a lazy Sunday afternoon at one of the many lakes around Jubilee, with the Blue Ridge Mountains towering in the background. It was so quiet and peaceful in those places. Just the two of them, often not talking for long stretches of time, and the occasional calling of a crow or screeching of a hawk flying overhead.

She missed the times he taught her how to make the perfect biscuit in the diner's kitchen. He said the secret was using a glass to shape them. He had always been her rock, her protector. Now, he felt like a stranger or someone she had to defend herself against.

She began writing again.

The argument we had today was bad. I hate fighting with him more than anything. It feels like I'm losing him a little more every time. I wish he could see that this isn't about taking sides. I'm not against him. I'm not trying to hurt him. I just want to follow my dream. But how can I do that when the one person whose opinion matters the most doesn't believe in me?

Her hand trembled as she wrote the last sentence. She set her pen down, letting out a shaky breath, and pressed her hands against her eyes, willing herself not to cry.

"This isn't helping," she said to herself. "You teach people how to handle stress, Whitney. Practice what you preach. Focusing on the negative isn't going to help anything."

She picked up her tea and took a slow sip, letting the warmth spread through her body. Then she closed her eyes and took in a deep breath, holding it for a moment before releasing it. She repeated that a few more times, focusing on the sound of her breath. People didn't realize just how much breathing correctly and taking time to breathe at all could improve their lives.

She sat there for a few moments, feeling the couch beneath her and the weight of the warm mug in her hands. When she finally felt a little bit calmer, she opened her eyes and went back to her journal.

A thought came to her, so she reached for her pen again.

This isn't just about Daddy. It's about me.

She stared at those words for a moment. Were they true? What did that mean exactly? Sometimes, thoughts came out when she wrote them, but they didn't come out when she only thought about them, so she began writing again.

I have always cared so much about what he thinks. I've always wanted to make him proud. But what about making myself proud? What about my own dreams? Isn't that just as important as what he thinks? Maybe more? I've spent so much time trying to meet his expectations. It's exhausting. I love him, but I can't keep living my life for him. I have to live it for me. And if someone truly loves you, they love all of you, even the parts they don't agree with or understand.

Her shoulders relaxed as she wrote the words. She continued.

My wellness studio isn't just a business idea. It's what I'm passionate about. It's what I believe in. Helping people feel better and live better—that's what I do. If Daddy can't see that right now, then I'll just have to show him. I'll prove to him that this isn't a waste of time, that it's worth it. And I'll prove it to myself, too.

She set the pen down again and leaned back, closing her eyes. She couldn't control her father's feelings or his actions, but she could control her own.

After finishing her tea, she closed the journal and set it aside. The world suddenly didn't feel quite so heavy. She wasn't sure how she and her father were going to find their way back to each other, but she knew that they would somehow.

She stood and walked to the window, looking out at the darkened street of Jubilee. The world outside was still and calm, and she wanted to find that inside of herself.

"I'll figure this out," she said softly. "One way or another, I'll figure it out."

Living alone meant that she talked to herself quite a bit. She turned off the light and headed to her bedroom, her mind spinning with ideas for her business's next steps.

Because for now, she was going to focus on herself.

And for tonight, she would allow herself to get some rest.

CHAPTER 10

Madeline pulled into the gravel parking lot of Jubilee Firehouse #2, her car crunching to a stop as she turned off the engine. In the passenger seat, she looked at the large paper bag she had brought with her. It was stuffed to the brim with sandwiches and chips, and a jug of sweet tea from one of the local restaurants was balanced precariously on the edge of the seat.

Her heart fluttered at the thought of seeing Brady, as it always did. It wasn't like she didn't see him all the time, but every time she did, it did something to her. Her ex-husband never made her feel that way. She was thankful to get to feel this kind of love at least once in her life.

She grabbed the bag and the jug of tea, juggling them awkwardly as she walked up the concrete steps and pushed open the glass door. The scent of stale coffee and faint traces of smoke greeted her as she walked inside, and the sound of hearty laughter echoed down the hall.

The firehouse was simple. Its walls were lined with framed photos of past crews, and a giant whiteboard displayed the day's schedule. She followed the sound of voices to the kitchen area, where a group of firefighters sat around a table, making jokes and ribbing each other like brothers—because they were.

Brady was among them, leaning back in his chair with his arms crossed. A grin lit up his beautiful face as he listened to one of the men tell a story. His deep and genuine laugh sent warmth through her chest.

"Hey there, boys," Madeline said, walking into the room. "I come bearing gifts."

The men turned toward her, their expressions instantly brightening.

"Well, look who it is," one of them called, standing up and grabbing the bag from her hands. "Madeline, you're a saint. Brady, you're one lucky guy."

"Don't I know it," Brady said, standing and walking over. He leaned down to kiss her on the cheek, his hand resting on the small of her back. "What's all this?"

"Well, I thought y'all might could use a good

lunch. I made some chicken salad sandwiches, brought some chips, and there's sweet tea, of course."

"You didn't have to do all that," Brady said.

"I wanted to. I know you guys have been working hard on all of these brush fires. I'll be glad when we get some well-needed rain."

The crew wasted no time diving into the food, passing around the sandwiches, and pouring cups of tea. Madeline stood back and watched as Brady effortlessly bantered with his co-workers. He seemed so at ease here and had so much cama-raderie, and she was glad because when he worked at the farm, he was often alone doing all of those tasks, and it was a lot.

Brady needed friendships, and he had lots of them. Everyone loved him. She couldn't think of anyone in town who had ever said a bad word about him, but they probably wouldn't say that to her anyway, given that she was his biggest fan.

Beneath her smile, as she watched them, was a knot of worry that twisted in her stomach. He'd been spending so much more time here lately because of the growing number of calls from the unusually dry weather. Every time he suited up and climbed into a fire truck, her heart clenched in fear.

"Madeline," one of the men said, "you make a

mean chicken salad sandwich. Brady, you better hold on to this one."

"Oh, I plan to," Brady said, winking at her.

She felt butterflies in her stomach. He looked so happy and so strong, but she couldn't shake the unease that followed her every time he went out on a call. Of course, she had never really told him that—not in so many words. She never wanted to take something from him that he enjoyed, that he felt called to do. That wasn't right. She would hate if anyone had ever told her to stop writing books.

The laughter died down, and the men were busy cleaning up, so Brady walked over to her, a knowing look in his eyes.

"You're quiet," he said, his voice low. "What's on your mind?"

She hesitated. "I'm just so worried about you. You've been here so much lately, and with all these fires happening, I can't help but think about all the things that could go wrong."

His expression softened, and he reached for her hand, his thumb brushing gently over her knuckles.

"Madeline, I've been doing this a long time. I know what I'm doing."

"I know that," she said, her voice cracking slightly. "But knowing how to do something doesn't make it easier. I mean, every time I know that I'm doing something wrong, it's—"

Before she could finish, the piercing sound of a station alarm cut through the air, followed by a dispatcher's voice coming over the speaker.

"All units respond to a brush and structure fire near 427 Maple Grove Road. Residential, flames visible, possible occupants inside."

The room sprang to life in a way that Madeline had never seen. The men all moved with purpose, grabbing their gear and heading straight toward the trucks.

Madeline froze, her heart racing faster than she'd ever felt it. "No," she whispered. "This sounds serious. Can't someone else go?"

He shook his head, his face set in determination. "This is what I do, Madeline. I have to go."

"Brady, please," she begged, grabbing his arm. "What if something happens to you? What if—"

He pulled her aside, out of the chaos of the kitchen, and cupped her face in his hands.

"Now you listen to me," he said firmly, his eyes locking with hers. "This is my town—our town—and these are our people. And if there's a chance somebody's in that house, I have to go. You know that."

Tears welled in her eyes, but she nodded. She could never ask him to be anything other than he was. A strong Southern gentleman, a hero in everything he did.

"I promise I'll be careful, as I always am. I promise I'll come back to you."

Her hands trembled as she reached up to touch his face. "You better," she whispered.

He kissed her then, a deep, lingering kiss that left her breathless, although it was short because he had to run. She was desperate to hold on to him for just a little longer.

"I love you," she said as he pulled away.

"I love you too," he replied, his thumb brushing away a stray tear from her cheek. "I'll see you soon."

And then he was gone, grabbing his helmet and running toward the fire truck. She stood frozen as she watched it roar to life and speed out of the station, its sirens wailing as it moved into the distance.

Alone now, she sank into a chair, her hands trembling as she tried to steady her breathing. The knot in her stomach tightened as she imagined all the things that could go wrong, but she reminded herself who Brady was. A protector of everyone. A fighter. A man who would do whatever it took to keep everyone in his town safe.

But she couldn't shake the fear.

All she could do was wait, her heart heavy with worry and love.

Whitney stood inside the entrance of Jubilee Vegan Cafe, holding her clipboard tightly. Her heart raced as she looked around the room, taking in the transformed space. Tables and chairs had been pushed to the walls to make room for yoga mats and meditation cushions. There was a small health station set up in the corner, complete with a blood pressure monitor and pamphlets about mindfulness. Tate's signature touch was evident with the snack station, where he had colorful platters of roasted vegetables, fresh fruit, and quinoa bites artfully arranged.

She pulled on her blouse, wishing it could calm her nerves. This was her big moment.

"You know, you're going to wear a hole in my floor if you don't stop that pacing," Tate said, stepping beside her with a smile.

She looked at him nervously. "What if nobody shows up?"

"They're gonna show up," he said, his voice calm and reassuring. "Listen, I've been seeing people read that flyer outside all day. They're curious, Whitney. Trust me, this is going to be a big success."

She inhaled deeply and exhaled slowly, trying to take her own advice about breathing. "Okay," she said, mostly to herself.

He reached out and gave her shoulder a gentle squeeze. "You've got this. I'm here if you need anything."

Just then, somebody walked through the door, and Whitney turned to greet her first guests. It was a middle-aged couple walking in hesitantly, looking around with curiosity.

"Hi, welcome," Whitney said, stepping forward with a bright smile. It occurred to her that she might be smiling too big, and she didn't want to scare people off. "Thanks for coming to Wellness Night. I'm Whitney Cooper."

The woman smiled back. "This is such a neat idea. We've been meaning to learn more about yoga and healthy eating."

"Well, you're in the right place," Whitney said, handing them a flyer with the night's schedule. "Feel free to grab some snacks or check out the meditation corner while we wait for others to arrive."

More people trickled in, and Whitney found herself bouncing between stations, introducing herself and answering questions. Every time she looked up, Tate was there, refilling the platters or chatting with people—a steady and comforting presence through the whole thing.

The door jingled, and Whitney felt even more at ease when she saw Madeline walk in, followed by Clemmy.

"Madeline!" Whitney rushed over, pulling her into a hug. "You came."

"Of course I came," Madeline said. "I wouldn't miss this for the world. Besides, I needed a distraction. Brady's on a call, and I've just been worrying myself sick all evening."

"I'm so glad you're here, then," Whitney said. "This is the perfect place to relax for a bit."

Clemmy, who was already looking around the room, set down her yoga mat. "Well, I hope there's room for an old gal like me," she said with a wink.

"There's always room for you, Clemmy."

"Good, because I need some serious enlightenment tonight. And don't worry, I'll be taking notes for the book club. You'll be the talk of Jubilee by morning."

Madeline chuckled and nudged Whitney. "You've got some big cheerleaders here tonight. Geneva wanted to come, but she's been a little under the weather with a cold."

"Oh no, I'm sorry to hear that. I'll be sure to stop

by with some special tea I have for just that sort of thing," Whitney said.

The room started to fill up, and Whitney's nerves slowly began to fade. She took her place at the front of the room.

"Hey, everybody," she said, her voice trembling slightly. "Thank you so much for coming to Wellness Night. I'm Whitney Cooper, and I'm so excited to share some simple ideas on how we can all take small steps to live healthier lives."

She looked over at Tate, who stood near the snack station, and offered an encouraging nod.

"So, for our first session, we're going to focus on mindfulness and meditation. Now, I know a lot of people think meditation is very woo-woo and something kind of out there, but all it is is about being present and giving yourself permission to be in the moment. It's not about clearing your mind completely because, honestly, that's impossible for most of us."

She led the group through some simple breathing exercises. Madeline sat with her eyes closed and followed along, her hands resting in her lap. Clemmy, who was sitting cross-legged, peeked one eye open and smirked when she saw Whitney looking at her.

"Now remember," Whitney said, "you can practice this anywhere—at home, at work, even if you're stuck in traffic. Of course, don't close your eyes if you're moving. It's all about finding a moment of calm in your day."

When the exercise ended, Madeline leaned over and whispered to Whitney, "That was exactly what I needed. Thank you."

Whitney smiled and then moved to the health station, where she took blood pressure readings for anyone who wanted one.

"Your numbers look good," Whitney said to a woman in her 60s. "But, you know, if you're interested, I have some pamphlets here with tips on how to maintain a healthy heart."

"Thank you, dear," the woman said. "This is wonderful, what you're doing here."

Whitney turned to look out the window for a moment and froze. Across the street in the darkness, she saw her father standing behind the counter of the diner, his arms crossed as he stared directly at the cafe.

"Everything okay?" Tate's voice brought her back to the present moment.

"Yeah, I'm fine."

He studied her for a moment before walking

closer. "You're doing amazing, Whitney. Don't let anything or anyone make you feel otherwise."

"Tate, what is this quinoa magic? I need the recipe immediately," Clemmy called out from the snack table.

Tate laughed and walked to her. "It's all in the seasoning, Clemmy. I'll have to write it down for you before you leave."

Whitney took a moment to compose herself, then moved to check on Madeline, who was chatting with a couple of guests.

"Feeling any better?" Whitney asked, sitting beside her.

Madeline nodded. "That breathing exercise helped, but I just can't stop thinking about Brady. I guess it was different because I happened to be at the firehouse when they got the call. Normally, he just leaves my house or wherever we are, and I don't really see the chaos that ensues when one of these calls happens. I'm nervous every time he goes out, but that one just really shook me."

Whitney placed a comforting hand on her arm. "Let's try something else. Close your eyes."

Madeline hesitated but eventually closed her eyes.

"Okay, now," Whitney continued, her voice

soothing, "I want you to picture Brady coming home safe. Imagine him walking through the front door. He's smiling, carrying some flowers, telling you everything's okay. Now, hold on to that image."

Madeline's lips curved into a smile. "That helps," she whispered.

"Good," Whitney said. "You've got this, Madeline. He's going to be okay. Anytime you worry about him, I want you to close your eyes again, take a few deep breaths, and see that image. See his smile, hear his voice, smell his cologne."

Madeline smiled. "I love the smell of his cologne."

The night continued with more guests stopping by, sampling Tate's healthy snacks, and chatting with Whitney about all sorts of things. When the evening wound down, Whitney stood near the front window again, watching as everybody trickled out. Across the street, the lights in the diner were dim, and her father was nowhere to be seen.

"You did it," Tate said.

She turned to him. "We did it."

"No," he said, his voice firm. "This was you, Whitney. All I did was make a few snacks. You were incredible."

For a moment, the world outside faded away, and all she could see was him.

"Whitney!" Clemmy's voice shattered the moment as she appeared with her purse slung over her shoulder. "Don't let this man hog all of your attention. I need to know when the next wellness night's happening. I've got ideas," she said, grinning.

Whitney laughed. "I'll keep you posted, Clemmy. I promise."

"Maybe we can host one at the bookstore," Clemmy said as she opened the door.

"Maybe," Whitney said, waving as Clemmy and Madeline walked out and down the road.

"You're going to change this whole town," Tate said quietly.

"I hope so," she said, "but not without a little help."

"Well, you'll always have help from me," Tate said.

Madeline stood beside her bed, tying her robe over her pajamas. She was going through her regular nightly ritual, trying to forget that Brady was fighting a fire. She washed her makeup off, brushed her teeth, and was now smoothing moisturizer onto her skin. The older she got, the more important that seemed to be. But tonight, everything felt so different

She picked up her phone on the bathroom counter and checked it for the tenth time in as many minutes. No messages, no missed calls. She knew better than to try to reach out. Brady was in the middle of a fire; he wouldn't even have his phone on him, and he certainly wouldn't have time to text her or answer a phone call. She sighed, turned off her bathroom light, and stepped into the bedroom. Even though the mountain air outside her window was still and quiet, she knew there was chaos surrounding Brady out there somewhere. The dry weather had made conditions so much worse, and every second he spent fighting that fire was another second she wished he was anywhere else.

She moved around the room, turning off the lights, her mind racing. She answered a text from her mother, who was still in Pigeon Forge, having a good time on her trip. Maybe she should have stayed at Wellness Night longer. Maybe she should have asked Whitney to just spend the night at her house and keep her calm. Being around Whitney and Clemmy had helped distract her at least for a little while, but now that she was alone, she was suffocating under the worry.

Madeline sat on the edge of her bed, holding her phone in both hands. She tried so hard not to let herself fall too deeply in love with Brady, but he had made that impossible. He had torn through every defense she had, and now the thought of something happening to him was unbearable.

The sudden, sharp ringing of her phone shattered the silence, and she nearly dropped it in her lap. Her pulse spiked as she fumbled to answer the call.

"Hello?" she said, her voice trembling.

"Madeline?" a male voice responded. She recognized it immediately as one of Brady's co-workers she'd met at the firehouse.

"Yeah, this is Madeline." She clutched her phone so tightly, she was afraid it might break.

"I'm calling about Brady. There's no easy way to say this. He's been injured."

Madeline's breath caught in her throat, and she struggled to make words. "Oh my gosh, what happened? Is he okay?"

"He was rescuing a child from one of the houses near the fire line. He got the kid out, but a big burning branch collapsed, and he was hit. He's been taken to Jubilee Memorial, and that's all I know."

Madeline felt her knees go weak. "Oh my gosh, I have to go. Thank you for letting me know," she managed to say. "I'm on my way there."

Her hands shook as she ended the call. She didn't even register what she was doing as she grabbed her purse and keys from the dresser. Adrenaline was surging through her, overriding anything else. She slipped on her shoes and threw on a jacket, not even bothering to remember that she was wearing her pajamas. Who cared? She had to get to that hospital as quickly as possible.

Her thoughts were consumed with Brady. All she could see was his smile, hear his laugh, and now the man who had come to mean so much to her was lying in a hospital, hurt and alone. She bolted down the steps and out to the car, the cool night air hitting her in the face, but she barely felt it. She climbed into the driver's seat, started the engine, and backed out of the driveway faster than she ever had before.

The mountain road stretched out before her, dark and winding. Her headlights illuminated the trees on either side. The tires skidded slightly on sharper curves, and she gripped the wheel.

"Stay calm," she whispered to herself. "You need to stay calm."

Her mind raced with every terrible possibility. Was he alive? Was he conscious? Was he in pain? What if this was worse than she could even imagine? For a brief moment, she considered calling Brady's sister, Jasmine. But Jasmine was out of town with her daughter, finally getting some much-needed time away. She didn't want to ruin their trip—not unless it was absolutely necessary.

"I'll just wait," Madeline said aloud to herself. "I'll wait until I know more."

Her foot pressed harder on the gas pedal, the car picking up speed. The hospital wasn't far now. Images of Brady filled her mind as she drove. She thought about the way he always held her hand when they walked together, the way his Southern drawl softened when he called her "darling," and the way he made her believe that she could do anything.

"You have to be okay," she whispered, gripping the wheel tighter. "You just have to be."

Finally, the hospital came into view, its lights shining like a beacon in the dark. She pulled into the parking lot, barely registering even where she was. She parked crooked, yanked the keys out of the ignition, and threw open the door. As she ran toward the entrance, her heart pounded in her chest like a jackhammer.

The automatic doors slid open right before she ran into them, and the cool, sterile air of the hospital greeted her like a slap in the face. She didn't even let herself catch her breath. She approached the front desk, her voice trembling.

"I'm here for Brady Nolan. He's a firefighter. He was brought in after an injury." She was speaking so fast, she was surprised the woman could even understand what she said.

The receptionist looked calm and professional. "One moment, ma'am. Let me check."

Madeline stood there, her hands gripping the edge of the counter. Every second she waited felt like an eternity. Finally, the woman looked up.

"He's in the emergency department. Take the elevators to the second floor and check in at the desk there."

"Thank you," Madeline said, running toward the elevators. She pressed the button repeatedly, willing the doors to open faster, and when they finally did, she stepped inside and jabbed the button for the second floor. She saw her reflection on the shiny elevator walls. She was pale, wide-eyed, and wearing her pajamas, which she only now realized.

"Please," she whispered to herself, "please let him be okay."

The elevator dinged, and the doors slid open. She stepped out quickly and approached the emergency department desk.

"I'm here for Brady Nolan."

The nurse behind the desk gave her a sympathetic look. "I'll let the doctor know you're here. Have a seat, and someone will come speak to you."

Madeline nodded, but she didn't sit down. She couldn't. She stood near the waiting room entrance, her arms crossed tightly over her chest. She didn't know how she could possibly keep herself from falling apart. Brady was here somewhere. He had to be alive, but until she saw him until she knew for sure that he was okay, the worry was going to gnaw away at her until she was bits and pieces on the floor.

CHAPTER 11

Whitney crossed the street toward Coop's Home Cookin'. Her Wellness Night had wrapped up, and she was feeling excited, literally buzzing from the success of the evening, but her heart was still heavy with the tension between her and her father. She stopped for a moment on the sidewalk in front of the diner, the familiar sight of the neon sign glowing faintly in the window. This place had been her father's pride and joy for as long as she could remember. It almost felt like her sibling, but today it felt like the diner had become a wall between them.

She took a deep breath and pushed open the door. It was very quiet in the diner. Even when they were closed or between shifts, it was never this quiet. Normally, she would hear the clanging of pots and pans or her father watching his TV in his little office in the back. At this time of night, he should have been cleaning up, stacking chairs, or counting the till. Instead, it was fairly silent.

"Daddy?" she called out, her voice echoing through the stillness.

No response.

The diner felt eerily empty. The soft hum of the fluorescent lights that she wished he would replace was the only sound she could hear. She stepped further inside, looking around the room. All the booths were clean, the tables wiped down, but the smell of today's fried chicken still lingered in the air. She looked over at the counter where Wanda's purse sat next to a stack of syrup dispensers. She relaxed a little, assuming Wanda was still here somewhere finishing up.

"Wanda?" she called out again, but there was still no answer.

Whitney stepped behind the counter and moved toward the kitchen. The lights were still on, which wasn't unusual for her father, but the silence bothered her.

"Daddy?" she called again, her voice more urgent now.

As she rounded the corner to the back hallway near his office, her heart dropped.

"Daddy?" she screamed, rushing toward him.

Coop lay on the floor, his legs sprawled out, and one hand clutched his chest. His face was pale, and beads of sweat glistened on his forehead.

"No, no, no," Whitney whispered, dropping onto her knees beside him. She grabbed his hand and tried to rouse him. "Daddy, wake up. Please wake up."

Behind her, she heard the sound of footsteps rushing toward her. Wanda appeared, her face alarmed.

"Oh my Lord, Coop," Wanda gasped, her hand covering her mouth.

"Call 911!" Whitney yelled. "Hurry!"

Wanda scrambled for her phone, dialing as fast as her fingers could move. Whitney turned back to her father. His breathing was shallow, but his eyes fluttered open for a brief moment.

"Whitney," he said softly, his voice raspy.

"Daddy, I'm here," she said. "It's gonna be okay. Help is on the way." She checked his vitals quickly. His pulse was more faint than she liked and definitely a lot slower than normal.

Wanda's voice echoed in the background as she spoke to the 911 operator, giving them their location and Coop's symptoms. Whitney fought to keep her composure.

"Daddy, you're gonna be okay. Just hang on. Please hang on."

His lips moved, but no sound came out. His grip on her hand tightened for a moment before his eyes closed again.

"Daddy!" Whitney cried, panic flooding her body.

The sound of sirens in the distance brought a wave of relief. Help was coming. It was the perk of a small town to be able to get help so quickly. Wanda knelt beside her, putting a hand on her shoulder.

"He's a tough old bird, honey. He's going to pull through."

Whitney nodded, but her heart was pounding so hard it felt like it might burst straight out of her chest. She reached for her phone, fumbling as she quickly texted Tate.

> Daddy collapsed. Ambulance is coming. I'm so scared.

She hit send just as the paramedics burst through the front door. Every one of these guys knew her father. They ate there for breakfast almost every morning.

"Back here!" Wanda called out, waving them toward Coop.

The two EMTs rushed to Coop's side, their movements swift and efficient, and Whitney scrambled out of the way, her hands covering her mouth as she watched them in shock.

"Coop, can you hear me?" one of them asked.

"Blood pressure's low," the other said, pulling an oxygen mask out and placing it over Coop's face.

Whitney held on to Wanda's arm as if her legs might give out at any moment.

"Is he going to be okay?" she asked, to no one in particular. Even being in the medical field herself, she found that her training about staying calm went right out the window when it came to her dad.

"We're stabilizing him," the EMT said. "We need to get him to the hospital."

"Can I ride with him?" Whitney asked through tears.

"Only one person can come."

"Go, honey," Wanda urged, squeezing her shoulder. "I'll lock up here and follow in my car."

Whitney didn't hesitate. She grabbed her coat and purse, following the paramedics out to the ambulance. The sight of her father being loaded into it made her chest tighten. The ride to the hospital was a blur of flashing lights and the steady beeping of a heart monitor. Whitney held Coop's hand the entire time, whispering words of encouragement. She wasn't sure he could hear her.

"You're gonna be okay, Daddy," she said. "You

have to be. I need you. I'm sorry we've been arguing. Please be okay."

As the ambulance pulled into the emergency bay, Whitney's phone buzzed. She pulled it out and saw a message from Tate.

> I'm on my way. He'll be okay. Stay strong.

Her tears fell freely as she tucked the phone back into her pocket. For once in her life, she had someone to support her. Her dad had done that for so many years, but she'd never been blessed to have a partner. And even though she and Tate weren't dating, she could feel his support even from afar.

The paramedics wheeled Coop into the emergency room, and Whitney followed closely behind, her heart pounding with every step.

"Are you family?" a nurse asked as they pushed through the double doors.

"I'm his daughter."

"We'll update you as soon as we can. Please wait here," she said, motioning to the waiting area.

Whitney nodded numbly, her legs feeling like jelly as she sank into one of the chairs. She buried her face in her hands. Her father, the one constant in her whole life, was fighting for his life, and all she could do was wait and hope.

W hitney sat in one of the uncomfortable chairs in the ER waiting room, her leg bouncing with nervous energy. She hated the sterile white walls and the hum of the fluorescent lights, although she was used to them, working in the medical field herself. But right now, it just felt suffocating. She could smell the antiseptic that hung in the air, and the occasional sound of somebody being paged over the intercom only added to her anxiety. Every time she heard one of those pages, she assumed the worst about her father.

Her mind raced with every worst-case scenario she could think of. And again, being in the medical field didn't help in this situation. She knew too much.

She stared at the untouched cup of water in her hands, her fingers gripping it a little too tightly, bending the plastic. This couldn't be happening. Her father was indestructible, larger than life—until tonight.

She squeezed her eyes shut, but the image of her father lying on the floor of the diner just wouldn't leave.

"Whitney?"

She looked up to see Madeline standing a few

feet away, her face just as pale and her eyes red. Whitney straightened immediately.

"Madeline," she said, standing to hug her. "What are you doing here? Did you hear about my father?"

Madeline hugged her tightly and then pulled back.

"It's Brady," she said, her voice trembling. "He got hurt fighting a fire. They called me and said he was being brought here." She looked around the room, searching for any sign of him. "I don't know anything yet. They haven't told me if he's okay."

"You said something about your dad?"

"Oh, Madeline, I'm so sorry about Brady. I thought maybe that's why you were here." Whitney hesitated before continuing. "My dad collapsed."

Madeline slowly sat down in the chair, and Whitney followed.

"Oh my gosh," Madeline said softly. "I'm so sorry. Did you find him?"

"Yeah," Whitney said, her voice cracking. "I went over to talk to him, and he was barely conscious. I did everything I could do. I just hope it was enough."

"I'm so sorry," Madeline said, her own voice breaking. "I hate that we're both in this situation right now. The two men we love the most are somewhere in this hospital. I feel like I'm going to crawl out of my skin."

"Not knowing is the worst part," Whitney agreed.

For a moment, they sat in silence, the weight of their worries too heavy between them.

Madeline spoke first, her voice soft and shaky. "You know, he's my soulmate, Whitney. I know how it sounds, but it's true. I have never in my life loved anyone like I love Brady. I've had this whole second chance at life because of him, and now I don't even know..." Her voice suddenly cracked.

Whitney reached over and put her hand on Madeline's knee. "Don't think like that. Brady is the strongest guy I think I know. He'll pull through. You'll see."

Madeline let out a shaky breath. "I know he's strong, but this is fire. Fire's unpredictable, and I think this one was different. They said it spread so quickly because of the dryness and the wind. He was trying to save a kid. Of course, he was trying to save someone else because that's just who he is, and that's why I love him so much. But it's also why I'm sitting here right now, terrified."

Whitney nodded. "It's going to be okay. He's in good hands now, and he's not the kind of guy that's going to give up without a fight, just like my dad."

Madeline smiled weakly. "Listen to me over here talking about my problems when you've got your own. I'm so sorry that you had to see that happen to your dad. It must have been horrible."

"It was terrible. It was the worst thing I've ever seen, and I've seen a lot over the years. When I saw him on the floor, I almost threw up. They think it could be his heart, I think, or…" Whitney trailed off. "I don't know exactly what's going on."

"Oh, Whitney, it's going to be okay. Your dad's a tough old bird."

Whitney swallowed hard. "Wanda was going to come over here, but I told her not to come until we find out what's going on. She was there for me, but honestly, I didn't want her panicking while she was sitting right beside me, and I was panicking," she said, smiling slightly. "Me and my dad have been fighting so much lately. I feel like this is all my fault. He's been so stressed, and it's all because of me."

Madeline shook her head. "No, don't you do that to yourself. Coop is as stubborn as a mule, and you know it. This isn't your fault."

Whitney looked down at her hands. "He's always been my rock, you know? My mom passed when I was so young, and it was just the two of us taking on the world. He was everything. My mom, my dad, my best friend, and now I don't know if he's going to be here."

Madeline reached over and took her hand. "He's

going to be okay, just like Brady's going to be okay. We're both going to get through this together."

Whitney nodded, although her chest still felt unbearably tight. She opened her mouth to say something else when suddenly the waiting room door opened. Tate walked in with a cup of coffee in his hand and a look of determination on his face as he strode over to Whitney.

"I brought this for you," he said. "Figured you could use it."

Whitney took the cup gratefully. "Thanks, Tate. You didn't have to come all the way here."

"Of course I did," he said, sitting down in the chair beside her. "I'm not leaving until we know how he's doing."

Whitney turned toward Madeline. "Tate, this is Madeline. She's here for Brady."

Tate extended his hand. "Yeah, I've met Brady a couple of times, and I think I saw you at wellness night. He's a good guy. What's going on?"

"He's a volunteer firefighter, and he was hurt. I don't know exactly how severely," Madeline said, obviously trying not to cry.

"Well, if there's anything I can do, please let me know," Tate said.

"Thank you."

The three of them fell into a silence, the weight

of their worries filling the air. Whitney took a sip of her coffee.

Tate leaned forward slightly. "How are you holding up?"

She shrugged. "I don't know. I feel like a zombie. I'm just trying to hold it together, I guess."

"Well, you're doing great."

She looked at him, his steady presence calming her a bit. "Thank you for being here."

"Always," he said.

Always. What did that mean? She didn't have time to think about it. Her mind was focused firmly on her father.

"I just wish someone would tell me something, anything," Madeline said, standing up and pacing.

"They'll come out soon. No news is good news, right?" Tate said.

Madeline nodded. "I suppose so."

She sat back down, and they sat together in the quiet hum of the waiting room, the sounds of laughter, coughing, and quiet sobs from other families surrounding them.

Despite the fear and uncertainty, Whitney felt a small glimmer of hope. She wasn't alone, at least. She had Madeline and Tate, and together they would face whatever came next.

Madeline paced the small waiting room, unable to sit still, even though Tate and Whitney had gently reassured her that everything was going to be okay. Every muscle in her body was tight, and every thought in her mind was filled with worry. Her chest ached from not knowing exactly how Brady was doing. The nurse had briefly told her he was stable, which made her feel a little better, but what exactly did that mean? She really didn't know.

Whitney reached over and squeezed her arm. "Hey, he's going to be okay, Madeline. I just know it. Why don't you sit down and take it easy?"

Madeline forced a tight smile. "Thank you. I'll keep praying for your dad too, but right now, I just need to keep moving. I'm going to walk over here and look out the window for a minute, so can you keep me updated if you hear anything?"

Whitney nodded. "Of course, and if you need anything, just text me."

Before Madeline could reply, a nurse appeared in the doorway with a clipboard in hand. "Madeline?"

She nearly tripped over her own feet as she rushed to talk to the nurse. "That's me. Is he okay?"

The nurse smiled. "He's stable, and we're ready

for you to come back and see him. He's actually asking for you."

Madeline let out a shaky breath as her heart pounded in her chest. Relief washed over her like a wave. She turned to Whitney and smiled.

Whitney waved her hand. "Go."

Madeline followed the nurse down the long, brightly lit hallway, her heart hammering in her chest as the nurse updated her on Brady's condition. She hated the hospital's overwhelming antiseptic smell. The nurse finally stopped outside a room and gestured for her to go in. "Take your time," she said gently before stepping away.

Madeline walked through the door, her breath catching in her throat when she saw Brady lying there. His leg was elevated, wrapped in layers of bandages, and an IV line was hooked to his muscular arm. Despite everything, he smiled when he saw her, his face lighting up just as if he hadn't just been through hell.

"Hey, sweetie," he said, his voice warm but obviously tired.

She could see remnants of black soot on him from the fire. Tears immediately sprang to her eyes, and she hurried to his side, grabbing his hand and holding it tightly.

"Brady, oh my gosh. They just said you were

injured, and I've been losing my mind out there, worried about you."

He squeezed her hand weakly. "I'm sorry I worried you. I'm okay, promise. Just a little banged up. These things happen."

She let out a small laugh and brushed her hand over his hair. "A little banged up? Half your leg's wrapped up in the air, and I heard you might need physical therapy. That doesn't sound like a little banged up to me."

He sighed, looking down at his bandaged leg. "Yeah, I've got some second-degree burns on my calf. They're keeping an eye on it to make sure it doesn't get infected. I twisted my ankle pretty good, too, when I tripped over a tree root while carrying the little girl out of the fire."

Madeline's eyes widened. "You realize that sounds like something out of a movie. You saved a child."

He nodded. "Her house was right on the edge of the brush fire. The flames were spreading fast, and she was trapped inside. I couldn't leave her there. She was only five years old."

Tears spilled down Madeline's cheeks as she leaned down to kiss his forehead. "Of course, you couldn't leave her there because that's who you are, Brady. You would put yourself in danger for others over and over again. This has scared me to death. I don't ever want to go through this again. I don't ever want you to go through this again."

His expression softened, and he reached up to cup her face with his hand. "I'm sorry I worried you, Madeline. I hate that I scared you. I never wanted to do that, but I couldn't let that little girl stay in danger. It's just not who I am."

She nodded. "I know, and I'm so proud of you. I can't lose you, Brady. You mean everything to me."

"I'm not going anywhere, sweetie. I promise."

She leaned down and kissed him again, this time on the lips, pouring all her relief and love into the kiss. When she pulled back, she sniffled. "They said you'd need wound care and physical therapy," she said.

"Yeah, I'll be off duty for a while. The doctor said I'll need to keep the leg elevated and come in for checkups regularly. I may even need to use some crutches for a bit until my ankle heals. You're gonna have to help me feed Gilbert."

She nodded, laughing. "Well, you're gonna have to let me take care of you. No arguments."

"I wouldn't dream of arguing with you. Besides, I kind of like the idea of you fussing over me a little bit."

She laughed through her tears, then leaned down

and rested her head gently on his chest. His heart-beat was steady beneath her ear, and it was the most comforting thing she'd ever heard in her life.

"I love you so much, Brady," she whispered.

"I love you too, Madeline," he said, "more than I can ever put into any words."

They stayed like that for a while, with the chaos of the hospital fading into the background as they held on to each other. Despite all the uncertainty and fear, Madeline felt such a sense of gratitude. Brady was alive, and he was hers, and that was all that mattered.

After a while, she sat up and brushed a stray hair from his forehead. "I should probably let Jasmine know what's going on, but I didn't want to scare her until I knew you were okay."

He nodded. "She'll probably want to come back and help, but you don't have to tell her everything right now. Just let her know I'm okay."

Madeline nodded. "I will, but first I'm gonna sit right here and make sure you don't try to pull any other hero stunts from this bed."

"You've got it, boss," he said, saluting her.

As the night wore on, and Madeline laid next to him in the hospital bed, she held his hand and thanked every star in the sky that he was still with her.

CHAPTER 12

Whitney's hands shook as she walked down the hospital hallway toward her father's room. It had been hours since he'd been back there, and she wanted to see him with her own two eyes. Her nerves were as frayed as they had ever been. She'd barely been able to relax since the moment she found him on the floor of the diner.

By the time she reached the door, she had to pause for a moment just to collect herself.

A nurse exited the room, holding a tablet. "You must be Whitney. Your dad's awake and stable. You can go in."

"Thank you so much," Whitney said.

Pushing the door open, she saw her father sitting in the hospital bed, his face pale, his usually robust demeanor so subdued. The sight made her throat tighten. Coop, the man who had always seemed larger than life, suddenly looked so small.

"Hey, Daddy," she said, stepping inside.

He turned his head toward her. "Hey, kiddo." His voice was hoarse, but the gruffness she knew was still there.

She pulled up a chair beside his bed and sat down. For a moment, neither of them spoke.

"They say it was a hypertensive crisis," she said. "Your blood pressure went through the roof, and they're keeping you here to monitor it."

He nodded slowly. "Yeah, doctor's been lecturing me about it all morning, said I've been living like a ticking time bomb. Guess he's not wrong. They've been warning me about this for a long time."

She folded her hands in her lap. "Daddy, why didn't you tell me you weren't feeling well? You've been pushing yourself way too hard, and with the diner and the stress, it was bound to catch up with you. They also told me you've known about your type two diabetes for over a year now, and you haven't taken any medication for it."

He sighed heavily and looked at her. "I didn't want you to worry. You have enough on your plate without me adding to it. These are just old people problems."

She leaned forward. "You're my dad. Of course,

I'm gonna worry about you. But you not telling me doesn't make it go away. It just makes it worse, and then I find you on the floor."

He rubbed his hand over his face and shook his head.

"Now tell me about this diabetes. You've known for a while—over a year. Why didn't you tell me? I'm a nurse! You didn't do anything about it—no treatment, no medication."

"I didn't want to deal with it," he said, his voice defensive. "I figured if I ignored it, it'd go away. I didn't want to take more pills or change how I ate. The diner's my life, Whitney. It's who I am."

"Daddy, this isn't just about the diner. This is your life, your real, actual life. You're more than the diner. If you don't start taking your health seriously, you're gonna end up in the hospital again—or worse —and I can't take that. You're all I have."

He was silent for a long moment, his jaw tightening, his shoulders slumped. "I know," he said quietly. "Believe me, I know. I was lying there on that floor before you found me. It scared me, Whitney. I thought about your mama and how I promised her I'd take care of you, and now here I am, a dang fool who can't even take care of himself."

The mention of her mother made Whitney's chest ache. She placed her hand over his. "We both miss her every day, but she wouldn't want us to live like this—hurting, scared, not talking to each other."

"You're right, she wouldn't. She'd tell me to quit being a stubborn old goat and start listening to my daughter."

Whitney smiled, tears slipping down her cheeks. "She sure would, Daddy. I need you to listen to me now. I know we've been at odds lately, but every single thing I'm doing—the wellness studio, wellness night—it's not just for strangers. It's for people like you, people who need help taking control of their health before it's too late."

He was quiet, looking down at their hands. "How did it go? Wellness night, I mean. Did folks show up?"

She hesitated, surprised by the question. "It went really well. A lot of people came. We talked about yoga, nutrition, mindfulness. Tate made some amazing snacks that people really loved. I even helped some folks check their blood pressure and talked about managing stress. Meanwhile, I didn't know my own father was across the street, lying on the floor."

"Sounds like you made a difference."

"I think I did. And I want to help you, too. You don't have to do this alone. I can show you how to eat better, manage your blood sugar, and reduce stress. But you have to let me. You have to stop feeling like you know everything and I know nothing."

He looked up at her, his eyes filled with a mixture of pride and regret. "Boy, I've been a real pain, haven't I?"

She chuckled. "You've been the stubborn old mule, just like you said, but I love you anyway."

He gave a small smile, the first genuine one she'd seen on him in weeks. "I don't deserve you, kid, but I am proud of you, even if I don't always understand your dreams. You've got your mama's fire in you."

"Thank you, Daddy. That means more than you know."

They sat in silence for a moment, the tension between them finally easing. Whitney glanced at the door as it opened, and Tate stepped inside, holding two cups of coffee.

"I figured you could use a little liquid energy," he said, handing one to Whitney. He nodded at Coop. "Good to see you awake, Coop."

Coop grunted but nodded back. "Thanks for looking out for her tonight."

Tate smiled. "Well, that's no trouble at all. She's worth it. And she can look out for herself pretty good."

Whitney felt her cheeks flush as she took the

coffee. She looked at her father, who was watching the interaction with one raised eyebrow—the same one he used to use on her when she dated in high school and came home a little too late.

"I'll leave you two to talk," Tate said, stepping toward the door. "Let me know if you need anything, and I hope you feel better soon, Coop."

Whitney watched him go, then turned back to her father, who was smirking.

"What?" she asked.

"Oh, nothing," he said, leaning back against the pillows. "Just thinking maybe that fellow's not so bad after all."

Whitney rolled her eyes and smiled.

Whitney turned the burner off and looked at the contents of the saucepan in front of her. The plain grits looked anything but appetizing, and the hard-boiled egg that she'd carefully peeled sat on the side of the plate like some kind of afterthought. She sighed, knowing this was not the kind of breakfast her father would have chosen, but after the scare at the hospital, this was the reality he was going to have to face.

She carried the tray carefully, making her way

through the house to his bedroom. He was propped up against a mound of pillows, flipping through the TV channels with a sour expression. She knew her father—he would much rather be at work right now than letting Wanda run the restaurant.

The sight of him tugged at her heart. He looked older and more worn than she'd ever seen him.

"Morning, Daddy," she said.

"Morning," he said, grunting.

"I made you breakfast."

She set the tray down on his lap.

"What in God's green earth is this?" he said, looking at it with disdain.

"Grits and a boiled egg," Whitney said. "Simple, healthy, and exactly what the doctor recommended."

"Where's the butter and the bacon? This doesn't even look like real food," he said, poking at the grits.

Whitney folded her arms. "The butter and bacon are what got you here in the first place. You're going to have to make some big changes, Daddy. No more fried everything and drowning everything else in gravy. You've got to take care of yourself."

He scowled but didn't argue anymore. Instead, he speared the egg with his fork and took a bite. He chewed slowly, making a face like he'd just swallowed a mouthful of vinegar.

"Lord, this is a pitiful thing, Whitney."

She sighed and sat down on the edge of the bed. "I know it's not what you're used to, but you've got to give it a chance. Your body needs to heal. It needs some real nutrition, not just daily doses of grease and salt."

She was about to launch into another plea for him to take his health seriously when she heard a knock at the front door. She stood quickly, relieved to have an excuse to leave the room for a minute.

"I'll get it," she said, heading down the hall as if Coop was going to get it anyway.

The doctors had told her to watch him for a few days and ensure his health. She wouldn't be able to do this forever. She had a job, after all, and she was planning to open her wellness studio. But right now, it was all about her father.

When she opened the door, Tate stood on the porch, holding a covered dish. His smile was warm, but his presence immediately set her nerves on edge.

"Tate, what in the world are you doing here?" she asked, stepping onto the porch and closing the door behind her.

"I heard your dad came home this morning. I wanted to bring him something—something he might actually eat."

"This is not a good time," Whitney groaned. "You

know how he feels about you, and the last thing I need is for him to get all stressed out again."

Tate's expression softened. "Whitney, I'm not going to start trouble with your dad. I just want to help. Trust me, this food won't upset him. It might even convince him that eating healthy isn't so bad."

She hesitated, looking over her shoulder toward the house. "I don't know. He's already in a mood this morning."

Tate stepped closer, lowering his voice. "Please, Whit, just let me try. This is important to me—and to him. After what I went through with my grandma, I can't just sit by and do nothing. This is my second chance. Let me help him."

Her shoulders slumped. She knew how much this meant to Tate, and she also knew her father needed all the help he could get, even if he didn't want any of it.

"Fine," she said. "Wait here."

She walked back to Coop's room, bracing herself for his reaction. He looked up as she walked in, his fork hanging above the untouched grits.

"Who was it?"

"Tate," she said, her voice careful.

"What does he want?"

"He brought you some food," she said, sitting down on the edge of the bed again. "Healthy food.

He wants to show you that eating better does not have to mean eating plain grits for the rest of your life."

Coop's lips pressed into a thin line. "Well, I don't need charity from him."

"It's not charity," Whitney said firmly. "He cares, Daddy. Whether you believe it or not, he does, and he wants to help. And I think you should let him. So can you please just let him drop it off and be civil?"

He stared at her for a long moment before sighing. "Fine, but don't expect me to roll out a welcome mat. I'm only doing this because I would eat anything other than these grits right now."

Whitney went back to the door and gestured for Tate to come in.

"Hey, Coop," Tate said, nodding respectfully. "Good to see you home. Hope you're feeling a little better."

Coop grunted, his arms crossed over his chest.

Tate ignored the frosty reception and set the dish on the bedside table. "So, I made you a vegetable quiche. It's dairy-free, gluten-free, and packed with protein. I think you'll like it."

Coop raised his eyebrow. "Dairy-free and gluten-free? So something that rabbits would eat."

Whitney gave him a warning look, but Tate just

smiled. "Give it a try. If you hate it, I promise I'll never bring you anything again. Deal?"

Coop sighed and reluctantly picked up the fork. He cut a small piece of the quiche and put it in his mouth. For a moment, Whitney couldn't read his expression. Then, it softened slightly.

"Well?" Whitney prompted.

"It's not bad," Coop admitted.

Tate grinned. "Well, I'll take that as a big win."

Whitney thanked Tate and then followed him to the door, stepping outside with him for a moment.

"Thank you," she said quietly. "I think that actually meant something to him, but he would never admit it."

"I'm glad," Tate said.

On impulse, Whitney stepped forward and wrapped her arms around him in a quick hug.

"You're a good man, Tate Morgan," she said, pulling back.

He smiled down at her. "And you're an incredible woman, Whitney Cooper. Your dad's lucky to have you."

He winked at her and then walked down the steps toward his truck. Whitney felt lighter than she had in the last few days. Maybe her father was turning the corner.

Madeline stood in the kitchen, the smell of sizzling bacon and scrambled eggs filling the air. She flipped a piece of French toast in the pan and glanced at the clock, realizing she was hovering over Brady like a mother hen. She didn't care. After everything that had happened, the thought of Brady being hungry or needing anything at all was unbearable.

She'd never felt this way about anybody. This was probably the closest she had come to mothering someone, even if it was her own boyfriend.

With a tray full of breakfast—eggs, bacon, French toast, and a steaming cup of coffee—she made her way to the living room where Brady was propped up in his recliner. His injured leg was stretched out, wrapped tightly in a bandage with a soft quilt draped over him. He was flipping through the TV channels with the remote, looking far too relaxed for somebody who had almost died just 24 hours ago.

Well, maybe that was a little dramatic, but that was how she saw it.

"Breakfast is served," she announced, putting the tray on a rolling table and situating it in front of him.

He looked up and smiled. "You didn't have to do all this, you know. I could have just had some cereal."

"Cereal? After everything you've been through? Not a chance," Madeline said, sitting down in the chair next to him.

"You know, I'm not an invalid. I can still function, Madeline."

She waved her hand dismissively. "You just got out of the hospital. Humor me, okay?"

He laughed, picking up the fork and taking a bite of the eggs. "Well, I'm not going to complain because these are perfect."

Madeline leaned back against the chair and watched him eat. He seemed so calm, so completely unaffected by the fact that he had saved someone's life just the night before. She couldn't shake the image of him lying in the hospital bed, pale and in pain, or the fear that had clawed at her chest when she got the phone call.

"Need anything else?" she asked, fidgeting with the edge of the quilt.

"Madeline, you've already done enough. You've been up since early this morning. You even fed Gilbert. Sit down and relax for a minute, okay?"

"I *am* relaxing," she said, folding her hands in her lap.

"No, you're hovering," he said with a smirk.

"You're treating me like I'm going to keel over at any second. It's making me a little nervous."

She started to open her mouth in protest, but the words caught in her throat. She looked away, trying to hide the tears that were threatening to spill over.

"Hey," Brady said softly, setting down the fork and reaching for her hand. "What's going on?"

She shook her head, blinking quickly. "It's nothing, I'm fine."

"Madeline, talk to me."

She took a shaky breath and looked at him. "I was so scared, Brady. When I got that call, when they told me you'd been hurt, I didn't know if you were going to be okay. I didn't know if I was going to show up at the hospital and find out you'd passed away. I didn't know if I was going to lose you."

His face softened, and he squeezed her hand. "I'm fine, Madeline. I'm right here."

"I know, but I can't stop thinking about how close I came to losing you. I know you love being a firefighter, but I don't know how I'm supposed to *not* worry every single time you go out on a call now."

He reached over and cupped her cheek with his hand. "Madeline, I get it. I do. I hate that this scared you so much, but you have to know this is who I am. I like to help people. I like to be there when they need me. It's in my blood. I can't just walk away from that."

She covered his hand with hers, leaning into his touch. "I know that, and I love that about you, and I would never ask you to stop. But that doesn't make it any easier. You're my whole world. I can't imagine my life without you, Brady. I just need you to know that I'm always going to be worried, and I'm always going to hover."

He pulled her onto the arm of the recliner and wrapped his arms around her. She buried her face in his chest and let the tears fall freely while his hand stroked her hair.

"I'm not going anywhere, Madeline. I promise you I'll be careful. I'll do everything I can to stay safe, but I need you to trust me. I came home this time, and I'll come home every other time, so can you trust me?"

She nodded against his chest. "I can try."

"That's all I ask," he said, kissing the top of her head.

They sat like that for a while, with the TV murmuring in the background, and for the first time since the accident, Madeline felt a little bit of peace.

Eventually, Brady leaned back, tilting her face to look at him. "No more tears, okay? I'm going to be fine. You're going to be stuck with me for a long time—until I'm old and ugly and fat from these French toast breakfasts."

She smiled through her tears. "Well, good, because I'm not letting you go anywhere."

"Deal," he said with a grin, pulling her in for a kiss.

When they finally broke apart, she rested her head on his shoulder, her finger tracing lazy patterns on his chest.

"Now, are you going to let me finish this amazing breakfast, or are you going to keep fussing over me?" Brady asked.

"Fine, I guess I'll let you eat—for now."

"Good," he said, picking up the fork again. "Because I don't want to waste a single bite."

CHAPTER 13

C oop sat in his favorite worn recliner, the old thing groaning under his weight as he adjusted the footrest. His TV was on, tuned to some afternoon rerun of an old western movie, but he wasn't focusing on the screen. He was staring at his fingers as they idly traced the arm of one of the chairs, because his thoughts were on one thing he didn't want to admit. Right now, he felt utterly useless.

For decades, he'd spent every single day of his life at Coop's Home Cookin'. Even when he had a cold, even when he hurt his ankle that time, even when it was a holiday.

Across the room, his friend and co-worker Wanda sat perched on the edge of the couch with a crossword puzzle in her lap. She looked over at him every so often, watching him with a quiet observation that only someone who'd known him for so many years could manage.

"You know, Coop," she finally said, "you're lucky I'm such a good friend, because not everybody would sit here spending their whole day babysitting a grown man because he can't be trusted."

Coop grumbled, folding his arms. "I don't need babysitting. I told Whitney I'm fine. She just doesn't listen."

Wanda smirked. "Oh right, she doesn't listen. She's your daughter, isn't she? Both of you are as stubborn as mules."

Coop shot her a look. "I'm not stubborn. I'm practical. I'm decisive. I know what I want."

"Uh-huh," Wanda said, her tone dripping in sarcasm. She set the crossword puzzle aside and leaned forward. "You know what, Coop? I've been sitting here for over an hour, and you haven't said more than ten words. What's going on in that head of yours?"

"Nothing's going on," he said, his tone short. "I'm just tired of everybody acting like I'm some kind of fragile old man who can't take care of himself."

Wanda raised an eyebrow. "Oh, is that what this is? You're mad at the world because people care about you? That must be real hard, having a daughter and friends who want to see you stick around for a while, even if you drive us nuts."

Coop sighed. "It's not that. It's, I don't know, Wanda, things just feel off lately. Ever since Whitney started this whole wellness thing, I feel like she's pulling away. She's going to have a whole different life that doesn't include me. It's like she doesn't need me anymore.

Wanda stood up and crossed the room, sitting next to his recliner on the hearth.

"Coop, that girl needs you more than you realize. She always has, and she always will. But you know what? She's grown up, and that's what grown-up kids do. They start making their own choices. It doesn't mean she doesn't love her father."

Coop stared at the floor.

"Well, it doesn't feel like love when she was siding with Tate and leaving me out of everything. I've been her rock her whole life, Wanda. She's going off and doing her own thing, and what if she just doesn't need me anymore?"

"You know, Coop, I didn't talk to my oldest son for two years because of a silly fight. Two years, Coop, over nothing more than a difference of opinion. And you know what the fight was about?"

He looked up, shaking his head.

"He wanted to move to Florida with his wife and

kids. I didn't want them to go. It was all about me. That's all I was thinking about. I felt like they were abandoning me, like they didn't care about me anymore. So I got mad, dug my heels in the sand, said things I shouldn't have, and he left. Two whole years went by before I swallowed my pride and picked up the phone."

Coop leaned back in his chair.

"What happened when you called him?"

"He answered," Wanda said simply. "He'd just been waiting around for me to come around the whole time. Let me tell you, Coop, those two years were the loneliest times of my life. I'll never get that time back with my grandkids or my son, and it was my own fault. Don't let that happen with Whitney."

He rubbed his chin, his brow furrowed.

"You really think it's that simple, Wanda? What if I don't agree with some of what she's doing? What if I see her making mistakes? It's just not the life I imagined for her."

"It's not about the life that you imagined. It's about the life that she imagines for herself. And whether you like it or not, she's got every right to chase her dreams, just like you chased yours when you built that diner."

"So you think I've been a little too hard on her?"

She looked at him, giving him a look that said everything without having to say a word.

"I don't want to lose her, Wanda. I don't know how to let go of wanting what I think is best for her."

"You don't have to let go," she said softly. "You just have to keep your mouth shut. You have to trust her. She's a smart woman, Coop. You raised her that way. She's got a good head on her shoulders. She helps people every single day at that clinic. My friend Marcy had a terrible case of pneumonia, and Whitney was the one who got her back to health. I'm telling you, if you keep fighting her on this, you're going to push her away permanently. Trust me, it's a pain you don't want to feel."

Coop sat in silence for a moment, the sound of the TV filling the space. Then, he finally looked at Wanda, his eyes heavy with emotion.

"You don't think it's too late?"

She shook her head.

"It's never too late, Coop. But you have to be the one who takes the first step and supports her. Show her that you're willing to meet her where she is, and maybe, just maybe, you'll see that what she's doing isn't so bad after all."

"I'll think about it," he said, nodding slowly.

"Good, that's all I can ask." She stood up and grabbed her crossword puzzle from the couch.

"Now how about I fix us some coffee? That decaf nonsense Whitney keeps trying to make you drink isn't worth the ground it's brewed on, but I suppose we have no choice."

Coop chuckled. "Yeah, we don't have a choice."

Whitney stepped out of her car and pulled her cardigan tighter around her as the cool evening air swept over the square. She'd had a very long shift at the clinic. It seemed everybody in town was getting sick all of a sudden. She had stopped by the vegan cafe to thank Tate for what he'd done bringing her dad food. To her relief, Coop seemed to be making some small steps toward accepting the changes he needed to make. She thought that maybe that little hospital visit scared him straight, but she couldn't shake the feeling that Tate's gesture might have helped nudge him in the right direction.

The lights inside the cafe were dim, but she could see Tate through the glass wiping down the counters as he prepared to close for the night. She waited a moment, wondering if she was intruding, but then pushed the door open.

He looked up, a surprised smile breaking across his face.

"Whitney," he said, setting down his cloth. "What are you doing here? Is everything okay?"

"Everything's fine," she said, waving her hand. "Just wanted to say thank you. My dad, well, you know, he actually enjoyed the food you brought. Well, he didn't hate it. He's never going to admit that it was delicious or anything."

Tate's smile widened. "Just saying he didn't hate it is high praise coming from your dad."

She laughed softly. "It really is. You know, I think you might have done the impossible. You might have gotten through to him in a way that I couldn't."

He leaned against the counter. "I didn't do anything special. I just wanted him to know that it's not about taking things away from him. It's about adding something better to his life."

"Well, anyway, it meant a lot," she said. "To both of us."

Then, there was a pause, a silence that was heavy in the room. Whitney glanced at the clock on the wall.

"Well, I guess I should let you finish closing up. Just wanted to stop by and say thanks again." She turned toward the door, but Tate's voice stopped her.

"Hey, Whitney?"

She turned back. "Yeah?"

"Would you be interested in having dinner with me tonight?"

"Dinner?" she repeated, caught off guard.

"Yeah, you know, it's the last meal of the day."

Whitney laughed. "I know what dinner is."

"I know it's last minute, but you look like you've had a long day, and I thought maybe you could use a break."

"You know, I'd like that," she said.

Tate's face lit up. He walked over to the door and flipped the lock.

"Wait, where are we going?" she asked, watching him turn off the neon open sign.

He grinned, pulling the blinds down over the windows. "We're going right here. You look too tired to go anywhere, and I make a pretty decent chef."

"You're cooking for me here?"

"Why not?" he said, moving toward the kitchen. "You're always taking care of everyone else. Just let me take care of you for a change."

Her heart melted a little at his words. She found herself smiling as she sank into one of the booths.

"Well, okay then. You've got my attention. What's on the menu?"

"You'll just have to wait and see," he teased.

Whitney leaned back in her chair and allowed herself to relax for the first time all day. She watched as he moved around the kitchen through the door, his movements fluid and confident. The lights were dim, and there was a soft hum of music playing in the background.

A few minutes later, he came out of the kitchen with a small tablecloth and a candle, which he set in the center of the table. He lit the candle.

"Candlelight?" she said, raising an eyebrow. "Wow, you're really going all out?"

"For you? Always," he said, his voice low.

Whitney's breath caught in her throat, and she looked away, focusing on the flame instead of the intensity of his gaze. Tate returned to the kitchen, and soon, the air was filled with the aroma of roasted vegetables, garlic, and herbs. When he returned, he carried two plates, setting one in front of her with a flourish.

"Vegan mushroom risotto," he said, "and a side of roasted Brussels sprouts. I thought you'd appreciate something a little lighter after a long day."

Whitney stared at the plate, her mouth watering. "This looks incredible."

"Wait until you taste it," he said, taking the seat across from her.

She took a bite, and the creamy, rich flavors exploded on her tongue. "You weren't kidding. This is absolutely amazing."

"I'll take that as a compliment," he said, watching her with a smile.

They ate, and the conversation flowed easily, as it always did. Tate asked about her day at the clinic, and she asked him about his latest menu experiments. There was an obvious undercurrent of connection that neither one of them could deny.

When they finished eating, Tate cleared the plates and returned with two small bowls of fresh fruit drizzled with a honey-lime glaze.

"Dessert," he said.

"You've thought of everything, and you didn't even know I was coming."

"I hoped," he said, sitting down again.

She took a bite of the sweet, tangy fruit. Tate leaned forward with his elbows on the table.

"Whitney, there's something I need to say."

Her heart pounded in her chest. "Okay."

"I respect you so much," he said, his voice steady but vulnerable. "The way you care for people, the way you're chasing your dreams despite the pushback from your dad. It's incredible. And I feel like I'm falling for you."

She stared at him. He continued, his eyes searching hers.

"I don't know how you feel, but I needed to tell you because every time I'm around you, I feel like I found something I didn't even know I was looking for."

She felt her eyes welling with tears. She reached across the table and took his hand.

"Tate, I feel the same way. I've been so scared to admit it, even to myself. But you, well, you make me feel seen in a way I never have before."

Relief flickered across his face, followed by joy. He stood and pulled her to her feet. They stood there for a moment, the space between them charged with emotion. When he leaned in, she met him halfway. His lips were warm and soft against hers, and the kiss was slow and unhurried—a perfect blend of tenderness and passion. Her hand slid up to his shoulders, and he pulled her closer, one hand gently resting on the small of her back.

When they finally broke apart, she rested her forehead against his.

"You know, I could get used to this," she whispered.

"Do you mean the food or the kiss?" Tate asked.

"Both," she said.

Madeline hummed to herself as she carried a tray into the living room, balancing a steaming cup of coffee and a plate of scrambled eggs and jelly toast. Despite the cheerful light streaming through the windows of Brady's house, her heart felt heavy. She walked into the room where Brady sat propped up on the couch, his injured leg resting on a stack of pillows. His crutches leaned against the armrest, and he was staring at the TV, though it was clear he wasn't really watching it.

"Breakfast is served," she said brightly, setting the tray in front of him.

He offered a small smile. "Madeline, you don't have to keep doing this. I can get my own food."

"Not today, you can't," she said, hands on her hips. "The doctor's orders were clear after your last visit—rest and no weight on that leg unless absolutely necessary. That includes you hopping around the kitchen like a bunny rabbit."

He let out a sigh. "Fine. Really, you're fussing too much."

She wasn't used to hearing him speak so shortly to her, but she knew he was frustrated. She perched on the arm of the couch. "You know you're impossible. Just eat it before it gets cold."

He reached for the plate, but she noticed his movements were a little stiff. Brady was always so strong and self-reliant, and it was clear he was struggling with this loss of independence, even though it would only be short-lived. She watched as he picked up the food, his appetite not the same, especially with the painkillers he was taking when he needed them.

He tried to act like everything was fine.

"Brady," she said gently.

He didn't look up. "What?"

"You don't have to pretend for me. I know this is hard for you."

He set the plate down with a little more force than necessary. "I hate this, Madeline. Sitting here feeling useless. It's like I'm not even me anymore. I can't do anything around the farm. I can't help at the firehouse. I can't even go outside without worrying about tripping over these stupid crutches."

His voice cracked, and he leaned back against the couch, rubbing his face with his hands.

"Brady," she said softly.

He shook his head. "I'm sorry. I didn't mean to snap at you."

"I know," she said, scooting closer. "You're allowed to feel frustrated. You've been through a lot."

"I don't mean to take it out on you. You've been amazing. I don't know what I would do without you."

"That's what I'm here for, to help you. But you

have to let me. You don't always have to be strong. It's okay to lean on me."

"I'm not used to this, relying on someone else. It's hard."

"I know it is," she said, taking his hand. "But you don't have to do it alone. You've taken care of so many people for so long—your family, your friends, this entire town. It's okay to let somebody take care of you for a change."

The tension eased as he let out a breath. "I guess I don't really have a choice now, do I?"

She grinned. "No, not when I'm around, you don't."

Before either of them could say more, the front door suddenly burst open, and Brady's niece Anna's voice echoed through the house.

"Uncle Brady!" she yelled.

Madeline turned to see her bounding through the living room, her curls bouncing as she ran straight to the couch and climbed up beside him, wrapping her arms around his neck.

"Hey, kiddo," Brady said, his face lighting up. "What are you doing home so soon?"

Jasmine walked in behind her, carrying their luggage. "We cut the trip short," she said, hurrying to his side. "We heard what happened, and there's no way I was going to stay in Pigeon Forge and act like my brother wasn't injured on the sofa here."

"Jasmine, you didn't have to do that."

"Of course I did," she said, her voice shaking as she leaned down to hug him. "You scared the living daylights out of me, Brady. Don't you ever do that again."

"I'll try my best," he said, chuckling softly.

Anna pulled back, looking up at him with her wide eyes. "Mama said you saved a little girl from a fire. Is that true?"

He smiled, ruffling her hair. "I just did what I needed to do, sweetie. That's all."

"That means you're a hero," Anna said, her voice filled with awe.

Madeline felt her heart swell as she watched the interaction. Despite his frustration and pain, Brady was still the man she loved—kind, selfless, and devoted to the people he cared about.

Jasmine sat down beside Madeline, her hand resting on her knee. "How's he really doing?" she asked in a low voice.

"He's healing," Madeline said. "It'll take time, but you know he's strong. He'll get through this."

Jasmine nodded, her eyes filling with tears. "I don't know what I would have done without him,

Madeline," she said. "He's the glue that holds this family together."

Madeline squeezed her hand. "He's going to be okay. We'll make sure of it."

The two women shared a quiet moment as they watched Anna chatting with Brady, her youthful energy filling the room. They had a long road ahead, but as long as they all had each other, she knew they could face whatever came next.

CHAPTER 14

W hitney and Madeline walked arm-in-arm around the square. The late afternoon breeze carried the scent from the flower shop down the way, and the town buzzed with activity as locals ducked in and out of the stores.

"Man, I really needed this," Whitney said. "Between shifts at the clinic, helping Dad, and trying to plan my next move, I feel like I've barely had a moment to just breathe."

Madeline gave her a knowing smile. "You're doing so much, Whitney. Sometimes, a walk and good company are all you need to recharge. And, of course, I totally understand what you mean. Brady's been a little bit difficult because he doesn't like for someone to take care of him."

Whitney smiled. They both stopped to admire

the display in Frannie's bakery window, commenting on how they had both earned a slice of pie and planned to get one later.

As they turned the corner, Whitney suddenly froze mid-step.

"Wait a minute," she said, her gaze locking on a small storefront nestled between the bookstore and the boutique.

"What is it?" Madeline asked.

Whitney pointed to the glass door of the building, a newly hung sign that read *For Lease,* gleaming in the sunlight. The space looked modest but inviting, with large front windows that let in plenty of light. Whitney remembered that it had been an old insurance office, though it looked a bit worn and outdated.

"Madeline," Whitney whispered, "look at the space."

Madeline tilted her head. "It's cute. Is this the kind of place you've been looking for?"

Whitney nodded, stepping closer. "It's perfect. I mean, it needs some love, obviously, but look, it's right here in the heart of the square. Everybody would pass by it on their way to the shops, and those windows would be amazing for natural light during yoga classes."

Madeline smiled. "I can see the wheels turning in your brain already. What are you picturing?"

Whitney stepped up to the window, pressing her hands against the glass. She saw things that other people might overlook—a blank canvas waiting to be transformed. She could imagine the polished wood floors and softer lighting. She envisioned mats lined up neatly for yoga class, a cozy corner with chairs for her mindfulness workshops, or maybe even small desks for consultations.

"It could be everything," Whitney said, her voice filled with excitement. "Yoga, meditation, nutrition workshops. I could have a whole schedule of classes. And the windows are so inviting, people could see what's going on just walking by, and maybe they'd want to join in."

Madeline crossed her arms and grinned. "Well, it sounds like you've already moved in."

Whitney turned to her and smiled. "It's just a dream right now."

Madeline shook her head. "You've done a lot toward your dream already, Whitney. Wellness night was a big success, and the town is clearly ready for something like this. Call the number, find out the details. This dream of yours doesn't have to just live in your head."

Whitney hesitated and looked back at the sign.

"What if it's too expensive? What if it's not exactly what it seems, and I waste their time?"

"What if it works out great?" Madeline countered. "You'll never know unless you try, and you've got everybody rooting for you."

Whitney took a deep breath and pulled out her phone. "Okay," she said, dialing the number on the sign. "Let's see if this dream has any chance."

Madeline clapped her hands. "That's my girl."

Whitney adjusted the blood pressure cuff around her father's arm as he sat on her exam table at the clinic. Coop fidgeted, clearly uncomfortable.

"Daddy, would you stop squirming, please?" she said, tightening the cuff. "I can't get an accurate reading if you keep moving around."

He huffed but settled down. "Feels like I've been poked and prodded enough already. How much longer do we have to wait for the doctor?"

Whitney smirked. "You're the one who insisted on coming early to beat the rush, and now you're complaining?"

Coop muttered something under his breath, but she ignored him. His blood pressure had improved a lot since the hospital stay, and she felt a small sense of relief.

"Well, your numbers are better," she said, writing in his chart. "The medication seems to be helping."

"Good," Coop replied gruffly, "but I don't like taking pills every day."

Whitney gave him a look. "Daddy, we've been over this. This is not optional. Your health depends on it. I better not find out that you've stopped taking those pills."

Before he could respond, there was a knock at the door.

"That'll be Dr. Grant," Whitney said, but when nobody entered, she realized they'd still have to wait. She sat down for a few minutes on the stool beside him, tapping her pen against the clipboard.

"Since we have a few minutes," she began, her voice hesitant.

Coop raised an eyebrow. "What are you up to? You look like you're about to drop some bad news on me."

"It's not bad news," she said quickly. "Well, at least I don't think it is."

"Spit it out, Whit."

She took a deep breath. "I signed a lease on the storefront I told you about."

For a moment, Coop didn't respond. His face was

unreadable, and Whitney braced herself for the explosion. Instead, to her surprise, he smiled.

"You signed the lease?"

"I did," she said cautiously. "I know you're probably upset. I know you think I should just stay at the clinic or keep helping at the diner, but—"

"Whitney," he interrupted, holding up his hand, "stop. I'm proud of you."

Her mouth dropped open. "Wait, what?"

He chuckled. "You heard me. I realize I've been a stubborn old fool. I was so caught up in my own fears that I couldn't see just how much all of this meant to you. But after everything that's happened, I finally realized something."

"What's that?" she asked.

"We only get one shot at this life, and I was holding you back because I was scared. Scared you'd fail, scared you'd leave me, scared I'd lose you. But you know that's not fair to you, and it's definitely not the kind of man I want to be. So yeah, I'm proud of you, kid. I'm sorry if I've made this so much harder than it needed to be."

Whitney's throat tightened with emotion. "Daddy."

He reached out and patted her hand. "You don't have to say anything. Just know I'm always rooting for you, even if sometimes I don't understand what you're doing."

"And that means more than you'll ever know," she said, tears welling in her eyes.

"So, since you're in a supportive mood," Whitney said, her tone lightening, "how would you feel about becoming my first success story?"

"What do you mean by that?"

"Well, I mean," she said, sitting up straighter, "I think I can help you—not just with your diabetes and blood pressure, but with everything. I could show you how to eat healthier, help you come up with better options for the diner menu, teach you how to meditate, breathe, manage stress."

Coop held up a hand, looking overwhelmed. "Hold up just a minute. You're talking about a lot of changes here. I'm not sure I'm ready for all that."

"I'm not saying you have to do everything all at once. But if you let me help you, I think you'll see a big difference. Besides, you'll be helping me too. If I can show people how much this has helped you—the most stubborn man in town—it'll be the best advertisement for my new studio."

He scratched his head. "I don't know. I've been eating fried chicken and biscuits my whole life. You asking me to give that up?"

"Not give it up," she said, "just balance it out.

You'd be surprised how some of this healthy stuff can taste. Tate's been helping me figure it out, and you already like what he brought over the other day —and what you tried at his place."

Coop grumbled something under his breath. "Fine," he said. "I'll let you try. But don't expect me to turn into some kind of health nut overnight."

Whitney laughed. "Deal. One step at a time."

The door opened, and Dr. Grant stepped in, clipboard in hand. "Good afternoon, Coop," the doctor said. "How are we feeling today?"

Coop glanced at Whitney and then back at the doctor. "Better," he said. "Maybe I'm ready to start making some changes."

EPILOGUE

EIGHT WEEKS LATER

Whitney stood in the middle of her brand-new wellness studio, Mountainside Wellness, taking in the scene around her. The walls had been painted a soft, calming green, and framed prints of mountain landscapes and inspirational quotes dot the walls. The hardwood floors had been polished, and they gleamed under the soft lighting. Fresh flowers from the local florist decorated the small reception desk.

Her heart swelled as she looked out at the small crowd that had gathered for her grand opening. Friends, family, and familiar citizens from Jubilee filled the space—Madeline and Brady, Tate, of course, her father, Clemmy, Geneva, Frannie, and even Heather and Lanelle, who ran the local inn. So many people had meant so much to her throughout her life.

Everyone chatted and looked around the studio, sitting in the cozy nutrition classroom, smelling the fresh catering from Jubilee Vegan Cafe, and inspecting the yoga studio. It was such a warm and welcoming atmosphere that she couldn't wait to start coming to work here every day. She had cut down on her hours at the clinic, and if the wellness center really took off, then she would leave there for good.

"Hey, Whit, you ready?" Coop's voice came from behind her.

She turned to see her dad, looking healthier and more vibrant than he had in years. He had traded his typical diner apron for a nice button-down shirt and slacks, and while he still had his same stubborn streak from time to time, she could see the pride in his eyes.

"Almost," she said, smiling. "How are you feeling?"

"Well, you know, I'm better than I've been in years," he admitted. "I'm not saying I love all the green stuff you shove down my throat every day, but I'm getting used to it."

She laughed, nudging his arm. "That's good

because I'm about to tell the town just how far you've come and that you're going to be around for decades longer than you would have been, so they better get ready."

Coop grumbled, but a smile tugged at the corners of his mouth.

Just then, Tate appeared, carrying a tray of vegan hors d'oeuvres. He was wearing a dark blazer over a crisp shirt, and his usual laid-back demeanor was replaced with something a little more polished for the occasion.

"Room for one more snack table?" he asked.

"Always."

As Tate set the tray on the refreshment table, Whitney felt a gentle hand on her shoulder. She turned to see Madeline standing there, looking as radiant as ever.

"Everything looks amazing, Whitney," she said. "You've really outdone yourself."

"Thank you. I couldn't have done it without everybody supporting me."

Behind Madeline, Brady leaned against the door frame, his leg in a brace but a smile on his face. He waved at Whitney, giving her a thumbs up. As he nibbled on something from the snack table, Clemmy and Geneva were deep in conversation near the meditation area, their laughter echoing through the studio.

Even Wanda had come, standing by Coop with a proud expression on her face.

Whitney stepped up to the front of the room, tapping a glass with a spoon to get everybody's attention. Everyone quieted as all eyes turned to her.

"Hey, everyone," she said, trying to keep her voice steady despite all of the butterflies flying around in her stomach. "Thanks so much for coming today. This studio has been a dream of mine that I've talked about with a lot of you for a very long time. It wouldn't have been possible without the support of everybody in this incredible town, the people that I'm lucky enough to call my family and friends."

The crowd clapped, and she continued.

"Over the next few weeks, Mountainside Wellness will be offering yoga classes, mindfulness workshops, nutrition seminars, and so much more. My goal is to create a space in Jubilee where everyone feels welcome and supported in their journey to health and happiness."

She paused, her eyes landing on her father.

"And speaking of journeys, I want to share a little success story. My dad, Coop, has been working with me over the last eight weeks after a health incident that was very scary for both of us. I'm so proud to say that he has already lost fifteen pounds. He's brought his hemoglobin A1c down by two points, getting closer to being non-diabetic, and has learned how to manage his stress in ways I didn't even think were possible."

The crowd laughed as Coop raised a hand in mock surrender.

"All right, all right," he said. "Don't embarrass me too much, Whit."

Whitney grinned. "He's even been sneaking in some yoga stretches when he thinks no one's looking."

More laughter erupted, and Coop stepped forward, clearing his throat.

"Y'all know I usually don't make speeches," he said, his voice gruff but full of emotion. "But I just want to say how proud I am of my little girl. She's always been the light of my life, even when I've been too stubborn to admit when I was wrong. But what she's done here is incredible, and I'll be the first to admit also that this Tate guy over here isn't so bad after all."

The crowd clapped, and Tate chuckled, shaking Coop's hand. Whitney felt tears well in her eyes as she hugged her dad.

"Thank you," she whispered.

"Anything for my little girl," he said, smiling. "Also, I have some big news."

"Bigger than what you've already done with your health?"

"Yep. I realized that my life doesn't only have to be about work. So, I'm taking some time off. Gonna rent that RV I've always talked about and hit some fishing spots around North Carolina and Tennessee for a couple of months."

Whitney's mouth fell open. "Really? But what about the diner?"

He smiled as he waved Wanda over. "This lady right here is my hero. She's agreed to a promotion and is now the manager of Coop's Home Cookin'."

Whitney smiled. "Congratulations, Wanda!"

Wanda waved her hand. "Oh, Lord, girl. I don't know what I've gotten myself into."

"You'll do great!"

"You may have to come to help me from time to time," Wanda said, laughing.

Whitney shook her head. "Oh, no, I'm not!" she said, giggling. "Those days are over."

The crowd dispersed to explore the studio and eat the refreshments, and Tate appeared at Whitney's side.

"Come with me for a second," he said, his voice low.

Curious, Whitney followed him to the back of the studio. He reached into a bag, pulled out a framed photograph, and handed it to her.

She smiled. The picture, taken at sunset, beautifully frames the front of Mountainside Wellness, with the soft glow of her sign lighting up the square.

"Tate," she said, "this is beautiful."

He gestured to the corner of the frame where a small note was tucked. She pulled it out and read the simple handwritten words: *This is just the beginning.*

She looked up at him. "The beginning of what?"

He stepped closer, his eyes searching hers. "The beginning of your dream, your business, your life, and maybe the beginning of something else, if you'll let it be."

Whitney's breath hitched as he leaned in, his hand brushing her cheek. The world seemed to fade around them, leaving just the two of them in that moment, and then he kissed her. It was slow and sweet and full of promise, the kind of kiss that felt like the first step towards something extraordinary.

When they finally pulled apart, Whitney smiled up at him.

"This is definitely the beginning," she said softly.

Tate grinned and took her hand as they walked back in to join the celebration. Around them, laughter and warmth filled the air, the perfect reflection of a life that Whitney had always dreamed of building.

And now, at that moment, she knew with her dad by her side, her friends cheering her on, and Tate's hand in hers, anything was possible.

Download your FREE Jubilee welcome packet by typing in the link below. You'll get a bonus scene, recipes from Jubilee, adult coloring sheets, printable bookmarks & more!

Get it here: https://BookHip.com/XTBVPNA

Made in the USA
Coppell, TX
11 March 2025

46881139R10134